Jerome A. Anderson

Driftings in dreamland : Poems

Jerome A. Anderson

Driftings in dreamland : Poems

ISBN/EAN: 9783743383432

Manufactured in Europe, USA, Canada, Australia, Japa

Cover: Foto ©Andreas Hilbeck / pixelio.de

Manufactured and distributed by brebook publishing software
(www.brebook.com)

Jerome A. Anderson

Driftings in dreamland : Poems

DRIFTINGS

—IN—

DREAMLAND.

❧POEMS❧

—BY—

JEROME A. ANDERSON.

THE LOTUS PUBLISHING COMPANY,

1170 Market Street,

SAN FRANCISCO, CAL., DEC. 25, 1894.

INTRODUCTION.

In presenting this little volume of poems to the public, the writer makes no claim to the distinction of being a great, or even a minor, poet. He believes from the very depths of his being that all men are alike, and one, in essence ; and therefore, that all have the poetic faculty, either actually or potentially. To demonstrate this by striking a few chords to which the humblest and lowliest hearts can respond, the collection is published. The poems, almost without exception, were written while the author was quite young. Since then, other work for humanity which seemed more imperative has caused the cessation of any poetical attempts. Whether these youthful poems will ever be justified by the better work of maturer years, depends upon that other work assuming— or seeming to assume—a relatively lesser importance. But the writer believes there is sufficient merit in this volume to justify its publication; else it would not be done.

JEROME A. ANDERSON.

CONTENTS.

MISCELLANEOUS POEMS.

YOUTHFUL POEMS.

To my Three Daughters,

Ivy,

Jessamine and

Violet,

This Book is Affectionately Dedicated.

MYSTIC POEMS.

REINCARNATION.

And in that far-off time, of which thou tellest,
   Thou shalt be I? When I am cold and dead,
And life from my numb fingers slipped and fallen,
   Thou shalt take up again its silver thread?

Thou shalt be I? My very dreams and visions,
   My hopes, my aspirations, and my fears,
My sins and shame—e'en these be in thy being,
   And mold thy fate through those thy span of years?

Nay, I had thought when this brief life is over
   To lay the body, like a worn-out tool, aside,
And the dark record of its earthly errors
   Within the silence of the grave to hide.

Or that the grave-earth through the coming ages
   Shut in and closed the Book of Life for aye.
And, say'st thou, there are yet unopened pages,
   And every page a life—another I?

So be it. There are thoughts my soul has cherished
   I fain would see live on when I am dead.

---

*A monologue, in which the reflected " I " of the present personality addresses the reflected " I," of the next. In the philosophy of Reincarnation, the real " I," the Reincarnating Ego, is untouched and unchanged by birth or death. With its lower reflection in matter, or each personal " I," the case is different. This perishes as an entity at death, and only lives in the memory of the Higher or Reincarnating Ego thereafter. Of course, it is the same " I am I" in each personality; but this poem is written from the point of view of the ordinary person, who has no recollection of preceding lives, and to whom, therefore, each life seems separate and distinct.

If but the good survived !   If evil perished
   Thou had'st not such a thorny path to tread.

And so, I charge thee, hearken to my warning,
   For I have somehow missed the goal in life,
And thou, mine other self, mayhap may'st profit
   By these my failures in its war and strife.

*   *   *   *   *

I have dreamed dreams of bold and high endeavor ;
   Of battles for the Right fought well—and won ;
Of succor for the oppressed ; of freedom conquered
   For serfs of every clime beneath the sun.

Yet, in the passion of the battle's clamor,
   I have been reckless of my thrusts and blows,
And oft have found, when passed the glamour fatal,
   Myself, a traitor, fighting for my foes.

And often when the world, mad, drunk with error,
   Knelt to some transient idol of its heart,
Crying, "Great is Baal ! Baal, live forever !"
   I have been silent : played the coward's part.

But thou—O, thou shalt see with clearer vision !
   Thou shalt face sternly, in majestic wrath,
All forms of error.   Fears shall not assail thee,
   Nor Doubt's dark demons stalk about thy path.

*   *   *   *   *

And if, amidst the warfare and the turmoil,
   The Sphynx has looked upon me, gloomy-eyed,

And questioned : "What is life?" I turned me priestward,
 And on their pattered creeds alone relied.

And if Christ's tender, pitiful forgiveness
 Seemed an unmanly portal to the rights
Of blissful heaven ; if such cheap salvation
 A warrant seemed for lengthening sin's delights ;

Or if pure Buddha's life-long sacrificing
 Of all desires that make our earth lives sweet
Seemed but a darkening of the holy wisdom
 That chains in flesh our erring, straying feet ;

Or if the sacred fire of Zoroaster
 Concealed the true Fire from our longing eyes ;
Or if Mahomet's holy fasts and vigils
 Led to a sensuous, selfish Paradise,

I questioned not. Thou shalt not need to question:
 All faiths shall yield their mysteries to thee.
Thou shalt lay bare the Secret of the Ages,
 And know the truth : and it shall make thee free.

The world has known a thousand holy Saviours—
 Each Judas-kissed, betrayed, and thrice denied.
Prometheus, Indra, Christna, Mithra, Jesus,
 Are but a tithe of these, its Crucified.

And thou shalt love them all. Thy larger wisdom
 Beneath each creed shall find truth's hidden gems.
Thou shalt ascend to many mystic Calvaries ;
 Thou shalt bring myrrh to many Bethlehems.

The separate goal, the personal salvation,
  Shall seem a selfish end to thy pure eyes.
Humanity's great, pulsing soul be thy soul,
  To perish with it, or with it to rise.

    *   *   *   *   *

And I have dreamed of love; and, in my dreaming,
  Have likened it to that rejected stone
Which made the temple perfect.   Blessed and radiant,
  Life crowned by love sits king-like on its throne.

Yet, like the treasure by some earth-gnome guarded,
  Love vanishes when just within our grasp.
Like Dead Sea fruit, it turns to dust and ashes—
  A Cleopatra's basket, with its asp.

And why?   Men know not love from selfish passion:
  They force, like Titus, its most holy shrine,
And find naught there but solitude and silence.
  Love dwells within: it has no carnal sign.

The love that seeks as its supremest object
  To crown another life with its high grace
Encounters lust, mad, frantic for possession,
  And dies in that unholy, fierce embrace !

And man who ever seeks some hapless idol,
  Forsaking stone, has made of woman one,
Wiser than He who first his help-meet fashioned
  Flesh of his very flesh ; bone of his bone.

Bone of his bone.   His strength, his weakness
  Is knit in every fibre of her heart,

In every good, in every sin or passion
　　Still is she help-meet; bears an equal part.

Except that man through ages of oppression
　　Has forced her to adopt a devious path;
Forbade to reason, taught to turn, dissemble,
　　She fawns and flatters to forestall his wrath.

He sternly bids her prophesy.　Her message,
　　Like Delphic priestess, in her cave of old,
Bears double meaning.　He in choosing
　　Takes that his self love wishes to be told.

And so she sits, a tottering, trembling goddess,
　　Upon the dizzy heights of her false throne.
Half conscious of her folly; half believing,
　　And wholly envious of man alone.

And yet her throne is formed of aspirations
　　Toward all that men hold sacred, holy, true.
She incarnates the virtues of the nations
　　As Buddha's ugly, lifeless idols do.

But in thy day—Oh, then shall love be perfect!
　　Thine eyes shall not be blinded by the light
Of fires unholy.　Thou shalt choose thine help-meet,
　　Star-eyed, clear-souled and radiant in thy sight.

She shall enfeminine thy harder nature;
　　Thou shalt bring strength where she is faint and weak
And thy divided lives shall this blessed union
　　Into the One of perfect being speak.

　　*　　　　*　　　　*　　　　*　　　　*

The weariness of age bears hard upon me,
  And memories of unforgiven sins
Loom large and black, as life's brief day declining
  Shows sharper shadows ere death's night begins.

And in my soul there dwells the gnawing sadness
  Of golden opportunities forever lost;
Of toils and pain to gain the gifts of Mammon;
  Of heaping dust to ashes, to my cost.

For I have lived for intellect; have wandered
  Down dusty paths of useless, cumbrous lore.
The surface-seeing, catalogueing Babel
  Of science I have held a priceless store.

That science which with all its store of knowledge
  Knows naught of life—from whence it came, or why.
A broken reed, it pierces, sharp and sudden,
  When at the end we lean on it to die.

    *   *   *   *   *

And I must wait (thou sayest) in worlds unreal,
  With earth's desires still hot within my heart,
While earth is not; and time and space together
  Forsake my life: become as things apart.

Yet feel the shock and thrill of mortal battles,
  While I seem by some hideous nightmare bound;
My touch unfelt, my form unseen, unnoticed;
  Voice my despair in shrieks that give no sound.

I shall press kisses on lips cold, unanswering;
  My loving words beat back on my own breath.

One hope alone shall cheer my fainting spirit—
  The speedy coming of the second Death.

One day is as a thousand years in His sight;
  A thousand years as one, brief, Summer day.
It well may be that one such hour of torture
  Shall purge a lifetime's earth-desires away.

Then I shall merge my purified existence
  Into bright visions, glorious, supreme.
The loved and lost shall gather close around me—
  I shall create and dream them in my dream.

And I will dream no partings there, no sorrows,
  (I shall be arbiter, creator, king),
No envy, malice, heartache, hate, ambition,
  No sin nor shame, nor any wicked thing.

Rest shall be there.   The moaning, tossing ocean
  Shall break no more its billows on the shore;
The laboring earth shall cease its fierce commotion,
  And storm and quake shall rend and throe no more.

And peace, and truth, and hope shall brood in silence,
  Until a new and perfect earth I tread.
The nations shall not gnash their teeth in anguish,
  Nor curse, nor murder, in their strife for bread.

Alas, the woes of life, its struggling, sinning,
  Are earth-born, of the body's fierce desire.
Few, few have sinned for knowledge or for wisdom.
  Soul sight grows clear at passion's funeral pyre.

And here the bitter struggle for existence
  Strengthens each base and false thing in our hearts,
Which else had died ; but now, in black luxuriance,
  Preys vampire-like upon our better parts.

Yet, while I dream, of wars and woes unconscious,
  The struggle for the Right will still go on.
Lo, even now, faint-limned against the Orient
  Appears the promise of the coming dawn.

Yea, champions shall rise ; and hairy Baptists,
  Shall cry out in life's wilderness of wrong ;
And Christ's shall come ; Buddhas forego Nirvana—
  And when I wake the time will not seem long.

Nay, when thou wakest.   I shall be forgotten
  When thou shalt "get thee coats of skin " again,
And joy in life with all its glorious newness,
  Unconscious of my old life's grief or pain.

My spirit shall be thine—I know it fully—
  Whate'er this mortal body may betide.
And yet, this brain that thinks, this heart so daring—
  They seem as kingly tools to cast aside.

Ah, well !   I merge my hopes and aspirations
  On thee ; and I will henceforth bring to thee
The sacrifice of all my lower nature
  That thou may'st rise, unfettered, fearless, free.

Thine eyes shall see the glory and the triumph,
  Thy lips shall voice the pæans and the songs,
When kingcraft, statecraft, priestcraft, all shall perish,
  And with them all their harpy brood of wrongs.

The petty aims of life, its vain ambitions,
  These are but toys that occupy its youth.
Its manhood's strength shall find but one vocation—
  The earnest, ceaseless search for God and truth.

*　　　*　　　*　　　*　　　*

Sometime these past lives all shall be remembered?
  Nay, then, if thou shalt gain that sunny height,
Look kindly back on this my feeble groping,
  Through doubts and darkness, towards the promised light

Perhaps the one, supreme, initial effort,
  The choice between the evil and the good,
That made thee possible, is marked by footprints
  Where my thorn-torn and bleeding feet have stood.

IN SHASTA'S SHADOW.

THE air is fragrant with the balmy breath
  Of stately cedar, and of drooping fir;
  Of mountain pines that softly sway and stir,
As each to each some whispered secret saith.

Above looms up great Shasta's hoary head,
  Clothed in white raiment of eternal snow.
  Silent, apart, he views the world below
Like one who counts his unreturning dead.

His birth-throes rent the reeling continents,
  'Midst shifting seas, and quaking, world-wide fears

When history closed her long account of years,
And turned a page, all white, for new events.

For when his peaks shook off the sapphire wave,
  And reared them haughty to the horrent sky,
  Atlantis sank, with drowning, dying cry,
To her abysmal, lost, forgotten grave.

Yet, since, he sits in lone, eternal pride;
  A civilization counts but one brief day;
  Its rise, its zenith, and its slow decay
Mark but a ripple on his life's long tide.

His wisdom is the fruit of age untold;
  His silence, because none can understand.
  Alone he sits, and, sphynx-like, views the land
Whose history is locked in his firm hold.

The Dwellers in the Caves—he saw their day;
  The Builders of the Mounds to him bowed down;
  The Aztecs sacrificed beneath his frown;
And these, the offspring of some lost Cathay—

All, all he knew.   Their long-forgotten past
  Lives in his memory, as fresh and green
  As these tall pines, whose leafy, emerald sheen
Begirts his base, in forests dense and vast.

Yet, like Atlantis, mayhap waits a sea,
  That shall o'erwhelm e'en his imperious brow.
  All things created to time's fiat bow,
And Shasta's very name shall buried be.

Still, ere that awful day, of nature's wrath,
  When she "repents" her having borne our race,
  And to our prayers turns stern, unpitying face,
While cataclysms sweep us from her path,

It may be Shasta, from his icy height,
  Shall look down o'er a happier, better world.
  Ormuzd, perchance, may win ; Ahriman hurled
Where new spheres rise by mingling wrong and right.

Then will the cruel race for wealth have ceased ;
  Ambition fold his bloody hands and die ;
  No Shylocks for their pounds of flesh shall cry ;
No idlers sit down to an unearned feast.

No more the war-cry of the strong be heard ;
  Nor nations plunged by king-craft into strife ;
  But in the new, grand Brotherhood of life
The deeper, truer chords of love be stirred.

Then Labor shall be king , unfettered thought
  Shall set his tasks to pure, harmonic song.
  Days shall be full of peace, and life be long,
And strife and evil cease, and be forgot.

O, Shasta, if before thou sink'st again
  Thou see'st these things, brought by our drifting ships,
  So shalt thou pass with blessings on thy lips,
And thy long life will not have been in vain !

RACHEL.

IN Ramah, o'er her infant dead,
   Wept Rachel; sore, uncomforted.

Above, the sky arched blue, serene;
Beneath, the vine-clad hills were green.

Soft breezes, fresh from Galilee,
Brought grateful kisses from the sea.

All fair things thronged about the spot;
Yet what availed when they were not?

The harp, swept o'er by fingers skilled,
Seemed mockery with their voices stilled.

The twitter of the nesting birds
Recalled their broken, childish words.

A thousand unexpected things
Brought sudden, sharp rememberings.

O, Jewess mother, centuries
Still echo thy despairing cries!

Thy life is not—is past, apart;
Yet still thy wailings haunt each heart.

Still we, who weep a withered flower
That bloomed one, transitory hour,

In our new grief but voice the woe
That wrung thy heart so long ago.

Still is the tear our eye that fills
Old as Judea's hoary hills.

And white lips mumble words of faith,
And each set phrase that comforteth.

But in our hearts, Death's "Dust to dust"
Meets voiceless plaint, "Unjust, unjust!"

And Time, who heals all wounds but death,
Folds helpless hands, nor answereth.

And so, like thee, with bowed head,
We mourn our dead, uncomforted!

AT THE END.

Some day shall death look on my face
And bid me follow to his place.

Some day my wearied lids shall seal
To earth, and awful things reveal.

What shall come first, of all that waits
Where life is barred back at his gates?

Will earth have fled, as flees a dream
Before the morning's 'wakening beam?

Or will our dim, sealed eyes, the end
The vision of enchantment lend

And earthly things change and grow clear,
Until we find that heaven is here?

Will slim, white hands we oft have kissed
Reach out and grasp ours through the mist?

And a soft voice, out of the Infinite,
Say, "Sorrow is dead, and woe with it."

"Of all sweet things in the vale of breath
There is naught so beautiful as death."

"Death, which you mortals so dread and fear,
Is a pitying, compassionate angel, dear!"

Ah, well!   Let us fold our hands and wait ;
Some day will be woven our web of fate.

And the Weaver shall look on it once and say,
"It is done as I planned it ; take it away!"

And the knowledge that no one can know and live
That moment under His eyes will give!

In the silence that follows ours souls shall hear
The Sphynx's dark riddle first made clear.

O, terrible joy!   O, moment grand!
To feel it is ours at last to command!

For life has concealed with the mists of his breath ;
But death must discover, or he is not death!

And we, who in life were the sport of fate,
At last his secrets must penetrate.

As dumb brutes we are constrained and compelled—
Life forced upon us and its meaning withheld;

But death, like a beautiful dream, ere long
Shall right each thing that has seemed to us wrong.

And our pale lips parted, but not with breath,
Shall whisper, "O, terrible, beautiful death,"

"Of your joys the chiefest, supremest good,
Is to find God knew; and we—misunderstood!"

FATE.

O, SULLEN SEA, that fling'st thy waves
    Against the adamantine rock,
Which age on age thy fury braves,
    Canst thou forbear the hopeless shock?

O brooklet, murmuring through the lea
    Where buttercups and pansies grow,
The gray, dead sea awaiteth thee,
    Yet canst thou stay thine onward flow?

O soul, that beatest 'gainst the bars
    Which gall and chafe thy prisoned life,
Defeat has marred a thousand wars,
    Yet canst thou cease the bootless strife?

REMINISCOR.

How sweet will earth life seem !
Who has not passed through troubled times, where foes
Made life a weary burden, till arose
Betimes strong friends, who stayed his sinking hands,
And victory wrought?   Yet when the shifting sands
Of life have thrown that barren waste of time
Far in the past, how discords melt to rhyme !
How do the false, the wrong fade from our view,
Leaving undimmed the good, the beautiful, the true,
    Blended as in a peaceful dream !

How sweet will earth life seem !
The sin and shame, the woe and misery,
Will all have faded.   Memory's drifting ships
Will cast the gall and wormwood in the sea,
And bring sweet wines alone unto our longing lips.
And we shall drink ; and with the draught shall come
Old earth life thronging back ; as passing sweet
As when in visions comes our childhood's home,
With grassy pathways for our tired feet,
With love our aching hearts to fill replete,
    And not one link lost from the perfect dream

REST.

O, DEAD, who slumber soft, with dim, sealed eyes.
    Nor struggle more for nature's hard-grudged breath,
  Is it not sweet, this solemn sleep of death,
Where tasks are done, and none cry out, "Arise?"

FAITH.

A traveller o'er a pathless plain
　　While yet from haunts of men afar,
Was shrouded by night's sable train,
　　Unlit by one faint, glimmering star.

Yet still he bravely struggled on,
　　Hoping to hold his course aright,
And soon a dim path chanced upon,
　　Which plainer grew as grew the night.

But when the morning dawned at last
　　To his amazement then he found
The long, long weary night had passed
　　Treading a narrow circle's round.

Oh, thus do men, with clinging faith,
　　Press onward through the night of life,
Each in his circle, until death
　　At last forbids the useless strife.

All faiths are false ; are but the track
　　Where wandering, erring feet have trod.
All faiths are true, for all lead back
　　To where we started—and to God.

ETERNAL PATIENCE.

In Egypt, godlike Cheops reigned,
　　And built a wondrous pyramid.
Long centuries have waxed and waned
　　Since in its depths his tomb he hid.

At length, by vandal hands laid bare,
  Some wheat grains in the tomb were found.
They sowed them there with wond'ring care
  In Gizeh's silent, sacred ground.

They sprouted, grew!   The cycling years
  Could not destroy the germs they hid.
Disturbed by neither doubts nor fears,
  They waited 'neath the pyramid.

Have faith, my soul!   The germs of good
  Somewhere within thy being lie;
The Bow of Promise spans the flood—
  Thine hour awaits thee, by-and-by!

MY CREED.

THIS is my creed: I cannot reach
  By thought, or word, or deed, the height
  Where God is throned.   My puny might
  Is less than naught in His pure sight.

Yet God made Man: and men are his.
  And so, like one who wandering
  Finds a poor brute, dumb, suffering,
  And succors the insensate thing

For love unto its master borne,
  E'en so towards man, frail, passion-tossed,
  Will I do right.   If, to my cost,
  More is required, then am I lost.

SEA SONGS.

THE SOUTHERN CROSS.

ATHWART a sky of purple dye
   It flared and flamed, a beacon light,
A grand, weird beacon, set on high
   To guide a drifting world aright.

And all around the restless sea
   White arms aloft did reach and toss,
And gladly called aloud to me,
   "The Southern Cross! The Southern Cross!"

And I was glad; and, gazing far
   Across the foam, blown white as floss,
I vowed no more the North's cold star
   Should lure me from this fiery Cross.

For that dear night she stood by me,
   My dark love, of the sunny South,
And each gust, eddying o'er the sea,
   Blew me sweet kisses from her mouth.

Her tresses, tangled by the breeze,
   Swept o'er my breast, in silken skeins.
Oh, never fetters dear as these
   Bound hopeless thrall in willing chains!

Her large, dark eyes now thrilled me through,
   Now drooped beneath their fringes long.
Her voice, low-toned, and accent true,
   Seemed sweet as some sad singer's song.

Clasped to my heart, with trembling joy,
　(How strangely kin are joy and pain!)
My happiness knew no alloy
　First, last, with thee, O maid of Spain!

*　　*　　*　　*　　*　　*

O, flaming Cross, far from thy sight
　I roam the icy North alone.
The love that dawned that starry night
　As dawned thy light for aye is gone.

And still I sigh, and moaning cry
　Unto the hungry, cruel sea,
O, give my sweet dead up to me
　O, sea, or clasp and bid me die!

SUNSET ON THE GOLDEN GATE.

FOAM-CRESTED waves, of molten gold,
　That rock enrapt in sundown beams,
　And hold and kiss the crimson gleams,
Like lover, grown with dalliance bold.

I list their murmur on the beach
　Of this, the wave-worn Occident,
　And muse if so the Orient
They lull with like low, dreamy speech.

Aye, speech of brighter skies than these,
　That look down o'er a fairer clime;
　A land of music, mirth and rhyme,
Of greener isles; of bluer seas.

For somewhere, while the billows fret,
  Rocks ship of mine, that rich freight brings
  To waiting me.   Their whisperings
Say, "Hold thy faith; she cometh yet!"

Still all they tell I can not ken—
  I know when South winds softly blow,
  And rippling crests, with murmur low,
Croon to their mates, who croon again,

That they are whispering of lands
  Which lie—I know not where; I list
  To voices, calling through the mist,
And fainting reach to reaching hands—

And suddenly my dream is gone.
  Returns the silvery beach once more,
  The crimson waves break on the shore,
And murmur on; and murmur on.

*   *   *   *   *   *

Now sinks the sun beneath the wave,
  And calls each lingering beam away,
  And speeds them forth, to herald day
On shores which Far-East oceans lave.

Reluctant yields each shivering crest
  Her lover, who in haste has fled:
  Yet blushing now a rosy red
That he so long lay on her breast.

But night, approaching silently,
  Hides now the blush 'neath purple pall,
  That falleth gently over all,
And lulls to sleep both land and sea.

AT SEA.

THE waves dash by with eager speed,
    As though from far-off seas had come
   Dim bugle call and roll of drum,
Telling of strife and hour of need.

And on each quivering, rushing crest
    The white foam leaps, like rider bold,
   Who, falling, yet regains his hold,
With lightest laugh when hardest pressed.

And gray gulls, folding weary wings,
    Alight within our vessel's wake,
   Drop far astern, then, rising, take
Our course, with scolding questionings.

To starboard glides a stately ship,
    With silent sails that glint and gleam;
   An utter stranger, yet abeam
Our courteous ensigns mutual dip.

And I—I look, and muse, and say,
    "O, brother, on life's stormy sea,
   Let this to us a token be
While threading our uncertain way."

"Reach out, and grasp my reaching hands
    For the brief time our pathways cross,
   Then though the waves roll in, and toss
Our barks apart, the moment stands.

An island green, whose emerald sheen
    Of wave-washed shores shall ever be
   A grateful, pleasant memory,
Tho' years and seas drift in between!"

SUNSET AT SEA.

OFF THE COAST OF SAN SALVADOR, CENTRAL AMERICA.

*A*WESTERN lies a weird, wide sheen
   Of waves, which stretch, a purple sedge,
  Out the far horizon's edge,
And droon and croon the waste between.

While to the East a tropic shore
   Looms out, as brought by magic wand;
  And seaward from the flower-strewn land,
Drift odors sweet, the waters o'er.

And farther back, within the marge
   Of shadows where creeps on the night,
  Dim outlined by his own red light,
Santana towers, black and large.

Anear, in moody silence, frown
   Huge peaks, whose fires have long since died;
  Yet grand they stand, in sullen pride,
Wrapped in the darkness, settling down.

Lo! in the West, as sinks the sun,
   A thousand viewless spirit hands
  Are busy, painting fairer lands
Than mortal eyes e'er look upon.

Dense banks of purple cloudlets form
   Dark foreground; then a crystal sea,
  A glassy, waveless, boundless lea,
Sweeps towards eternal shores; while warm

DRIFTINGS IN DREAMLAND.

And beautiful, a thousand isles
   Lie sparkling in the amber light,
   Gemmed o'er with verdure, fresh and bright
As April's inwreathed tears and smiles.

Through vales where star-crowned palm trees grow,
   A brook of gold steals soft, as if
   'Twere dazed, until from onyx cliff
It leaps into the sea below.

And crystal mountains rise, to mock
   Their compeers, black, upon the shore;
   These California's ruddy ore;
Of sapphire those, a solid rock !

Southward a fierce volcano burns,
   Outpouring lava, glowing, red,
   Which seeks a lakelet's emerald bed
And, cooling, into rubies turns.

And floating o'er the enchanted scene
   Are tinted clouds, fair as the mist
   Of colors, when by sunbeams kissed
The blushing rainbow's arc is seen.

But night creeps slowly, surely on—
   And somber grow the tints, and gray;
   Like earth hopes, fade they sad away,
And sea, and isles, and day are gone.

IN DIALECT.

IN THE DRIFT.

FAR away down the shaft, in the face of the drift,
    Two miners were busily working.
With a jest now and then, just to give time a lift,
As they toiled through the hours of the dreary night shift—
    Nor dreamed they of danger near lurking.

One Cornish. He spoke of his home o'er the sea,
    And its loved ones, with passionate yearning;
A dear, patient wife, who with hope ever bright
Watched o'er her three babes, kept the cottage aright,
    While awaiting the wanderer's returning.

How the thought fires his heart, puts new strength in his arm,
    And the worn drill is clanging and shrieking
At the quick, stinging blows which relentlessly fall,
Driving slow the hard steel in the firm granite wall,
    Which encases the treasure he's seeking.

The other, a mere lad, scarce out of his 'teens,
    Soft-voiced and fair as a maiden.
He had come from the States ; and he spoke of the day
When from mother and home he had wandered away
    To the mines, that with treasures were laden.

"And I never write back," added he, while his voice
    Grew cold, just to hide his regretting ;
"For I made up my mind not to write till I'd struck
Something grand ; but I never have had any luck,
    And I guess the old folks are fretting

To hear from me.　Well, I guess one of these days
　　　I'll sit down, and write them a letter
Just to tell them I'm living.　It's hard, tho', you see—
They always had counted so much upon me,
　　　And to think that I've not done no better!"

"Is the hole deep enough?　Well, let's tamp down the blast.
　　　It's too late to begin any sinking:
Stick a light to the fuse and come out o' that Joe;
We'll stop in the raise till we hear the blast go;
　　　It'll throw pretty well, I'm a-thinking."

　　　*　　　*　　　*　　　*　　　*

"A cave, did you say?　Great God, them poor men!"
　　　"Both killed, sir.　The boys say, what found 'em,
They were out in the raise, when the rocks overhead
Tumbled down, killing both the poor fellows stone dead,
　　　And pilin' the boulders up 'round 'em!"

"But the worst of all is, tho' we know very well
　　　How to write to the Cornishman's home,
Where the boy's folks are livin' can't even be guessed.—"
Ah, well.　After all, is it not for the best?
　　　They will die, still hoping he'll come!

FISHERMAN JOB.

"WELL, young 'un, you're mighty smooth spoken, and it all
　　　may be just as you say,
That God never interferes with us; but lets each one go on
　　　his own way;

But when heaven has silvered your locks with the snows of
    some eighty odd year,
As it has mine, and always in marcy, you'll regret this wild
    fancy, I fear.

"Just let me spin ye a yarn, sir, as happened a long time agone
To me, and if such is all luck, why, I hope it'll allus hold on.
It's now nearly three score Summers since this accident hap-
    pened to me;
Just after I'd married my wife, and settled down here by
    the sea.

"For I were a fisherman born, sir, lovin' always the wild
    waves to ride;
They're the type o' my life, an' I'm thinkin' that it's now near
    the turn o' the tide.
There were three of us then as were partners in the trimmest
    and best little boat
As ever were true to her colors, just a bright little "Sunbeam"
    afloat.

"We had had a long run o' good luck, sir, with the weather
    as fair as could be;
And the morrow were goin' again, when the gray light first
    dawned on the sea.
But, before I was fairly turned out it seemed as I heard
    something say,
'There's breakers ahead o' ye, Job; don't go on the sea, lad,
    to-day!'

"At fust I felt kind o' scared like, but I thought 'twas all
    fancy, you see;
So I took a good look at the sky; 'twas as clear and as bright
    as could be.

But it still seemed to whisper, 'Beware!' an' the breeze crept
    by soughin' and slow,
And a voice, like a wail for the dead, with each gust seemed
    to murmur, 'Don't go!'

"Then I got kind o' nettled, to think that my narves should
    sarve me that way,
An' I says to myself, 'You're an ass, Job; but ye'll go for all
    that, lad, this day.'
So I kissed wife a hasty good bye, and set off a hummin' a song,
'Till the path took a turn by that cliff, at whose foot the sand
    stretches along.

"Then what happened I never could tell, but the fust I re-
    member, I know,
The cliff were afrownin' above me, and I stunned and bruised,
    down below!
And my wife kneelin' down by my side, an' lookin' as fright-
    ened as if
I were dead. Says she, 'Job, were ye crazy? Ye walked
    right straight off o' the cliff!'

"I didn't say much; and of course my mates went out that
    day alone.
An' I lay on my bed, kind o' happy to find arter all I'd not
    gone.
But the strangest of all is yet comin', for that mornin' as fair
    as could be,
Was followed ere noon by a storm as was fairly terrific to see.

"We waited in agony, knowin' such a sea the boat could not
    outride;
And were thankful when even their bodies were laid at our
    feet by the tide.

It's no use in askin' my fate, if that mornin' I only had gone ;
And, if such things all happen by luck, why, I hope it'll allus
    hold on !

AUNT BEULAH

Why I never got married, Melissa ? Well, I'm sure I can't
    tell you, my dear ;
I haven't thought much about sweethearts for nigh onto
    thirty odd year.
I am sure I am happy, my darlin' that to-morrow will greet
    you a bride ;
But why I never got married—law, I never could tell, if I tried.

It wasn't that none came a-wooin', deary me I had plenty of
    beaux.
And more than I wanted. The right one didn't happen to
    come, I suppose.
Tell you about them ? You're foolish, my child. Let me see—
Well, the handsomest one, I remember, was curly-haired
    Robert McKee,

Did I love him ? Well, yes, child, he seemed once, of course,
    very dear ;
But, law, that has passed away long since, along with these
    thirty odd year.
Of course, I remember him yet, for we can't help that if we
    would ;
Though I never have tried to forget him, for there wasn't no
    reason I should.

And sometimes when I sit with my knittin' my thoughts
    wander back to the days
When I used to love spellins' and quiltins' and the parties,
    with old-fashioned plays.
And the sleigh bells that jingled so merry, as we dashed along
    over the snow,
For Robert at such times as these was generally with me you
    know.

And he seemed to be happiest always when he'd tucked me in
    for a ride;
And I wasn't quite so contented as when I was snug by his side.
Tho' we never said nothin', but only loved on in the old, quiet
    way;
But somehow I fancied that Robert grew dearer with every day.

Till one time that I long shall remember as the happiest hour
    of my life,
Came a letter that told all his love, and asked me to be his
    own wife !
Such a letter ! I always have kept it, tho' now it's so faded
    and blurred
That I scarcely can read it ; but then it was dearer than gold,
    every word !

So I stole me away to my chamber, to answer the letter, you see,
And tell him how happy I was to know that he loved only me.
Then I sent it ; and waited, and waited for his footsteps again
    at the door ;
And what there was wrong I don't know ; but I never saw
    Robert no more !

For the very next evening they told me he started across the
    wide sea ;

And I bore up bravely, to show them his goin' wan't nothing
to me.
But the sky for a time seemed so leaden, and the world was so
cheerless and cold,
And when it at last had passed over, I found I'd begun to
grow old.

For parties and spellin's and such things seemed to be kind o'
like children's play ;
And tho' there were many came wooin' there were none that I
cared to have stay.
So I've lived on contented and cheerful, and I can't say that
blessings I lack,
For I'm happy when gazin' before me, and I love, dearly love
to look back.

Cryin', child ? Well, joy that is deepest is oftenest seen in a tear ;
But for me it has passed away long since, along with these
thirty odd year.
I am happy, so happy, my darlin' that to-morrow will greet you
a bride ;
But, why I never got married, law, I never could tell, if I tried !

ONLY JOE.

This grave, were ye meanin', stranger ? Oh, there's nobody
much lies here ;
Its only poor Joe, a dazed lad ; been dead now better'n a year.
He were nobody's child, this Joe ; orphaned the hour of his
birth.

And simple and dazed all his life, yet the harmlessest critter
    on earth.

Some say that he died broken-hearted; but that is all nonsense,
    you know,
For a body could never do that as was simple and dazed, like
    Joe.
But I'll tell you the story, stranger, and then ye can readily
    see
How easy for some folks to fancy a thing that never could be.

Do ye see that grave over yonder? Well, our minister's daugh-
    ter lies there;
She were a regular beauty, and as good as she was fair.
She'd a nod and kind word for Joe, whenever she passed him by;
But, bless ye, that were nothin', she couldn't hurt even a fly.

It weren't very often, I reckon, that people a kind word would
    say,
For Joe was simple and stupid, and allus in somebody's way.
So when Milly took down with consumption or some such sick-
    ness as that,
Joe took on kind o' foolish—there were nothin' for him to cry at.

But when winter was come, she died; and I well remember
    the day
When we carried the little coffin to the old churchyard away.
It were so bitter cold we were glad when the grave was made;
And when we were done, and went home, I suppose poor Joe
    must have staid.
For they found him here the next mornin', lyin' close to the
    grave, they said;

And lookin' like he were asleep; but then, of course, he were
    dead.
I suppose he got chilled and sleepy, and how could a body know
How dangerous thet kind of sleep is, as never knowed nothin',
    like Joe?

ELIAB ELIEZER.

THE Reverend Eliab Eliezer
    Sat toasting his shins by the grate;
His ponderous brain busy musing
    On man's most pitiable state.

Abroad the storm-king was raging,
    And the snow was fast whitening the ground;
Yet its fury disturbed not Eliab,
    From his reverie, so deep and profound.

Aye; he thought how wicked and sinful
    Was poor fallen man, at the best;
And even Eliab Eliezer
    Was almost as bad as the rest;

And he piously groaned in the spirit
    At the flesh, which so leads us astray.
"There is nothing that's good," saith Eliab,
    "In these weak, worthless vessels of clay."

"Now there's swearing Meg, at the corner;
    Her case shows plainly, I think,

How wicked our natural hearts are ;
 How much lower than brutes we can sink.

" I will preach to my people a sermon,
 And take swearing Meg for my text,
And show them how narrow the safe road
 That leads from this world to the next."

So he sat himself down at his table,
 And began with " Original Sin ; "
And, by-and-by, Meg and her swearing
 Were deftly dove-tailed therein.

With thirdly and fourthly he finished ;
 Then turned to his grate, nice and warm ;
When he thought of Widow Morey, and wondered
 If she were prepared for the storm.

" I will call around soon in the morning
 And be sure that all is quite right."
He did ; and found food in abundance,
 And the grate with a fire glowing bright.

And the widow, with joy fairly weeping,
 Told how she was caught by the storm.
Not a morsel of food for her children ;
 Not a coal her poor hovel to warm.

And that they would surely have perished—
 Too chilled to go out and beg—
When pitying heaven sent succor
 By such a strange angel—old Meg !

Then a light slowly dawned on Eliab ;
    I can't say what conclusion he reached ;
But I know, stowed away 'mong his sermons,
    Lies one that never was preached.

LABORER MIKE.

MIKE earns just a dollar and a half every day,
    And toils from the rise to the set of the sun ;
He's a wife and five childer—the sixth on the way—
Who all have to eat and be clothed on his pay.
    Now, how in the de'il is it done ?

First, then, he burrows in some dirty street,
    In a basement, perhaps, or, perhaps, near the sky ;
And he pays forty cints every day to the cheat—
The landlord—God's vicar 'twould seem—the dead beat,
    But he's lord of poor Mike and his sty.

Two bits to the butcher for a bit aff the neck
    Of a sheep, for 'twill make both some broth and a stew ;
Potaties tin cints for the half av a peck ;
Siven mouths make of three loaves av bread a sad wreck,
    And that's fifteen cints, at the best you can do.

His groceries cost him some twinty cints more—
    For sugar and coffee and butter and sich ;
Thin tin cints for coal to cook his scant store ;
And tin cints for milk, av it's left at the door !
    And five cints for beer—wad ye grudge it, ye rich ?

So there's fifteen cints left for the clothes that they wear—
    For shoes, hats and coats, and such short-lasting things,
Four dollars a month, with a few cints to spare—
How the wife makes it do, we must niver inquire,
    For expadients laid bare is where poverty stings.

So Mike lives along, with nothing to fret,
    Till his job peters out, or the wife's taken sick;
Thin his bank suspinds payment, and Mike gets in debt
To butcher, and baker, and doctor, you bet,
    Just as long as each party will sell goods "on tick."

Thin what does he do? He finds a new job.
    But how can he live, and yet his debts pay?
He's a deep-thinking social economist, my bob;
He's honest at heart, and it hurts him to rob,
    So he gathers his traps, and—just moves away!

Pray, whose is the fault? Mike's labor is worth
    To some capitalist prince ten dollars a day.
He squanders the rest, for he's lord of the earth,
And he robs and cheats Mike from the hour of his birth,
    While we, heartless Levites, "pass by another way."

MISCELLANEOUS POEMS

LISSA.

PART I.

I have no thrilling tale to tell,
Of daring deed or awful woe;
And, should you follow where I go,
A wasted life is all I trace.
Its only merit, that I know,
A brother's 'tis, of our strange race.

LISSA.

I CAN not tell—I do not know,
    Though dumb, dead years have glided by,
Whose tombstones white, a ghostly sight,
Are all that now remain to show
I've lived them o'er,—I say, to me
'Tis yet an unsolved mystery
Why she should love me so ; or why
I gave such love again.   Aright
We can not read the future's lore—
The past is blurred by tears ; and we
Can only sigh; "Ah, me, Ah, me !
Sweet love is dead, to live no more !"

Yet this, and this alone I know,
Amid the wrecks the years have made,
We loved.   Trusting and unafraid,
We bade the fleeting moments go,
Believing, with unquestioning faith,
That equal joys the future hath
For those who wait with ne'er a doubt
To shut the Bow of Promise out !

Not beautiful ; but passing fair
She seemed.   A gold-brown, dreamy eye,
That haunts me yet, half pleadingly,
Half haughtily ; a wealth of hair
That rippled o'er her shoulders bare
In jetty curls ; and cherry lips,

Which stood half o'ped, in sweet surprise
That you should pass them idly by,
When they were waiting to be kissed,
If love would only claim his prize !

And oft I claimed it.   Never she
By word or sign opposed my will;
Yet still I durst not drink my fill
At such dear fountain, lest I be
With love intoxate grown, and bold
Had crushed my vase within my hold.
For deep down in her dreamy eye
I saw as plain as though it there
Were traced in words of fire, " Beware ;
That love which ever would endure
In its first state, untainted, pure,
Must veiled be by mystery !"

Such maid was she, as I have drawn
In colors all too wan and faint
Her shadow e'en to rightly paint
Who with firm, gentle grace, upon
Her throne within my heart reigned queen—
A worshiped queen.   And who was I,
That with such blind idolatry
Low at her feet was ever seen ?
God pity me ! I do not know—
I can not read the Sphynx-like book
Which opens when I inward look,
And mocks, and mystifies me so !

For I was aye a dreamer.   When
A wayward child, I roamed at will

O'er grassy vale, or wooded hill,
Sweet, strange companions with me then
Were ever present.   I could hear
Voices which reached no other ear.
Each violet blue or buttercup
Held elf, or shut a fairy up ;
A thousand leaflets, fluttering
With joy, to me were beckoning ;
Or else, if Autumn ruled the year,
And they had purple grown and sear,
So plain they told their tale of woe,
So mutely plead for grace to stay,
That I could almost weep, as slow
They trembling took their earthward way ;
While on the North wind's chilling breath—
Their slayer—they with touching faith,
Wafted a farewell piteously
To life, and light, to love and me.

Yet fairest seemed the bright Springtime,
When nature doffed her icy sheen,
And donned her beauteous robes of green ;
When in a happy, babbling rhyme,
A thousand voices sweetly sang,
A thousand echoes, answering,
Made 'wildering concord.   Low and clear,
Of all my sweethearts doubly dear,
The blushing flow'rets called to me
In love's own language.   Though there be
Long, silent years between, yet plain
I still can heart heir sweet refrain :

SONG.

Come, and kiss your sweethearts,
    Waiting, eager, longing ;
See us, laughing, pouting,
    Everywhere a-thronging.

Here are violets, nestling
    In bright, sunny crannies ;
Here are lowly daisies,
    Here, proud Jump-up-Johnnies.

Here are red, red roses,
    Regal in their splendor ;
Here are white, white lilies,
    Whispering, low and tender.

Buttercups and pansies,
    Brown-eyed, trembling clover—
All have kisses waiting
    For their ling'ring lover !

We, through dreary Winter
    Dared not show our faces,
So we've waited, waited,
    In our hiding places ;

Cruel, will you tell us
    That you did not miss us?
Out on such a lover—
    Hasten, kiss us, kiss us !

And love oft dies as flowers die,
Chilled by the North wind's icy breath.
Died ours by such cold, numbing death?
Nay; flowers can die by heat as well.
The very warmth which gave it birth,
And bade it grow and bud and bloom,
So oft the fragrant dew may sip
That sparkles on the lily's lip
As e'en to kiss it to its tomb.
Can love which burns thus fervently
Die by its own intensity?
It may be so; I can not tell.

In memory's halls the light falls fair
On one, the fairest picture there.
'Twas of a May-day, fresh and bright,
When happy, joyous lads and maids
Together met, 'neath sylvan shades,
To choose a sceptered Queen, whose right
To reign was peerless beauty's power.
How through my veins the hot blood raced,
When on her brow the crown they placed—
May's royal Queen, and fairest flower!
And low upon the bended knee,
In earnest half, half mockingly,
They vowed eternal fealty.
How song and dance and mirthful play
Ran riot through that happy day!
How each young pair, with guarded care,
To leafy nook would steal away,
And murmured vows and kisses rare
Would exchange there, on sweet May-day!

'Mid other schemes to while the time,
An acted play there lingers still,
Which, though but acting, sent a chill
Across my heart, like tolléd chime
Of bells, which clang out mournfully
With jarring grief, to feel that they
Must first the tidings sad convey
That Death again has laid his hand,
His ruthless hand, upon our band,
And ta'en from thence a dear-loved friend,
Whose face we never more shall see!

'Twas of a maiden young and fair,
With lover rare, of high degree,
Who humbly sued, on bended knee,
That she would hear and grant his prayer,
His loved and beauteous bride to be;
So well he plead that fain was she
To yield her heart unto his care,
When, suddenly, before them there,
Appeared a wrinkled hag, and old,
Whom all the people knew a witch,
On midnight jousts who rode her switch,
Who, to avenge some fancied wrong,
Over their hearts a glamour flung—
For passion pure deep hate upsprung;
Where love-fires burned were ashes cold!

To play the beauteous maiden's part
Was hers; and mine to humbly woo.
Oh, never seemed a farce so true
As this; or numbing to the heart.
No muttering witch whose curse-fraught tones
Rolled o'er love's tomb such heavy stones!

THE CHARM.

Fairies and elfins
    Peaceful or wrathful,
Tell, if ye ever
    Knew lover faithful !

Ye, who have witnessed
    Love's fiercest flashes,
Have they not ever
    Ended in ashes ?

Fickle is woman,
    Men are deceivers;
True love a myth, and
    Fools its believers !

A beauteous rose, with
    A worm at its center;
She who would cull it
    Soon shall repent her.

A chalice of crystal
    With joy overflowing;
A draught of its waters
    Contentment bestowing !

He who believes it
    As fair as its seeming,
Let him but taste it,
    And wake from his dreaming !

Aye, wake ; but to find him
    A slave ; doomed forever

To a hideous thralldom
Death only can sever !

Hast knelt where mourners gather 'round,
To do the last, sad rites of love,
On pallid brow the clods above
To place, and consecrate the ground
To death's long sleep ?   Oh, when the prayer,
The tearful prayer, breathed soft on air,
Hath ceased ; and stillness reigns profound
Till broken by the jarring sound
Of rattling clods upon the lid
Where all we love on earth lies hid,
Is not that sound an awful one ?
That shrouded sob, that muffled moan,
Heard in that stifling monotone ?
So seemed her voice that day, who laid
Grave earth upon my heart, nor stayed
Her hand till cold, damp tomb she made !

And gazing down on Lissa's face,
I saw hope, love and faith all fall
Beneath the spell, which like a pall
Enwrapped her, too, in its embrace.
And from that day where'er I fled,
I heard a clanging, tolléd knell,
That ever one sad tale did tell :
"Thy love is dead ; thy love is dead !"
The why—dumb lips can not declare ;
But how ?   Hast seen the tiny tongue
Of flame which in dry grass upsprung
When careless spark had fallen there ?
See, how it struggles for a hold—

A feeble thing a breath would slay ;
Ah, it has gone ! Nay, it has leaped
And caught another blade, which old
And dry, affords an easier prey.
Down to the root it now has crept,
And licks aloft, with tongue as red
As that which darts from cobra's head.
Yet stronger now a hundred fold,
It lurks, a widening sphere of gold,
Until it feels the fanning force
Of breath of air ; then on its course
It feebly starts—a beauteous thing !
But, see ! a thousand tongues upspring,
Which greedily dart far and wide,
And gather food on every side.

Down stoops the gale to nurse its wrath,
And urge it o'er its flaming path ;
And that which one short breath agone
Seemed e'en too weak to tread upon,
Now roars with hundred voices loud,
As wrapped within its flaming shroud,
It sweeps, a howling fiend, along !
An awful wall of fire ; its speed
By far outruns the swiftest steed.
Its wrathful roarings stun the ear ;
Its smoke, in columns dense and vast,
Pollutes and chokes the azure waste
Of heaven above ; its flames below
Leap, roar and crackle, like the glow
When fuel fresh in hell is cast !
The bellowing herds flee from its path,
And rush where water stays its wrath.

Before its rage men pale with fear,
As it licks up with greedy haste
The toil of years ; full happy they
If wife and babes are not its prey.

But it has gone ; and where before
A sea of grass, though brown and sear,
Waved beautiful the prairies o'er
Now but black, smoking wastes appear !

Thus died our love ; not cf my will,
Nor yet of hers ; but, helpless, we
Saw the wild heart-fiend first set free,
Watched his insatiate rage ; and still
Were powerless : and when at last
The bitter burning flames were passed,
And but dry, ashen plains remained,
We saw our love indeed was dead.
And cold and haughty then we spoke
Of that which was ; and there detained
Ourselves but till a grave we made—
Brief task—and love therein was laid.
Few were the sobs the silence broke,
And mocking prayers, if aught were said ;
And then to other skies I fled
And left the dead, and doubly dead !

LISSA.

—

PART II.

A song of blue mountains, which rear them aloft,
  In regions untrod, of our own Mexico;
Of beautiful brooks, that with murmurings soft,
  Bid adieu with regret, and awestering flow.
A ripple of waves where a brave ship glides;
  A moaning of surf on a tropical shore;
And Ever nor Never no longer divides
  Heart ashes from ashes long scattered before.

LISSA.

THERE is a land, as yet untrod
  By wandering, 'wildered feet of men,
Where mountain, valley, gorge and glen
Belong to nature—and to God.
For surely grander monuments
Of him who shaped this beauteous earth
Are not. The azure sky is rent
By snow-capped peaks, which reach aloft
In daring pride, as though in war
With heaven itself, their hands had torn
The veil that hangs between ; and hurled
Great granite masses to the sky,
Until where stars and planets are,
Where moons and meteors wander nigh,
They rear their haughty heads, in scorn
Of vanquished foe ; aye, pitch their tents
'Neath heaven's very battlements !

And prisoned valleys, far below
Lie nestling, in dumb, caged content.
Caged and yet free. For many a rent
Pierces the rugged mountain's side,
And yawns, a chasm bold and wide,
And deep and dizzy to the sight.
Yet still they lie, within the might
Of their strong conquerors ; whose hold
Is giant's grip, that grows not weak,
Tho' myriad crumbling voices speak
How grizzly gray they are, and old.

Amid grows tall the graceful pine,
With here a feathery, drooping fir,
And there a fragrant juniper.
And aspen dwarfs, which crowd to line
The marge of streamlet, welling out
The mountain's side.   These wait, in doubt,
With russet leaves that give no sign
Of their rich, beauteous design,
Until a breath one scarce could feel
Sets all a quiver with delight.
Then, with a flash like burnished steel,
Each turns its breast of silver white
Up to the sun's warm loving light.

And leafy pines and firs between,
Grows rich green grass, in matted swards,
So thick and dense as scarce awards
Room for the flowers.   These deck the sheen
Of waving green with many a star
Of golden hue, of violet blue,
Of flames that leap the darkness through,
Of silver and of amethyst,
Of myriad tints, which mock the mist
Of colors when the sun has kissed
And coaxed the blushing rainbow forth
From out her cloud-land hiding place
To gaze upon the beauteous earth.

Within the wood, the huge horned elk
Wanders, in all his antlered pride ;
While, on the sloping mountain's side,
Coy deer, in gray-blue coats of silk,
Loiter at will   In parks between

The fleet-limbed antelope are seen;
While far above, with hoof that rings,
From crag to crag the wild goat springs;
And, roaming restless far and near,
Like Satan 'mongst the Sons of Men,
Is found the giant grizzly.   He,
A mountain mass of ugliness,
Of hideous strength, and all beside
That spread his cruel terrors wide,
Is all the shadow darkening down
On land from wrath and wrong so free.

I wandered here till months had fled;
Alone I ranged the mountains o'er;
Dreamed new, strange dreams; learned mystic lore
From nature's page, so fair outspread.
I saw that God is good; that when
He, resting, said His works were good,
That they indeed were perfect.   Men
May turn blind eyes that will not see,
May point weak fingers, scoffingly,
But are alone in their vain pride.
The towering pine, so princely, grand,
Is fittest for the mountain's side;
But where, 'mid parched and fevered sand,
The cactus grows, fierce-barbed and mailed,
Not less a monument it stands
Of one design, that has not failed!

And, far above the petty strife,
Where each seems to himself control,
He sits; and molds each separate life
In one harmonious, perfect Whole.

His men are Empires; strong and great
They rise, live out their lives, and die;
Or weak and faint, they yield to fate
Ere seems begun their destiny.
Still with a strong hand and a just,
Omnipotent, except to fail,
His ends are served when they are dust.

One day it chanced I wandered far
From my accustomed paths; and stood
At eve upon a mountain's crest.
And, gazing out unto the West,
I felt within my veins the blood
Leap quick with gladness.   Like a star
I saw a distant, glimmering light
Far down beneath the chilly height,
And knew that I had neared again
The long-forsaken haunts of men.
The morrow I stood face to face
With a small fragment of a race
Through whom ran Montezuma's blood.
Gentle and trustful, they received
With welcoming hands the strange, white man,
And, nothing questioning, relieved
My wants, as due from man to man.

And I—I stood as in a dream,
And listened to their voices low,
And musical, as is the flow
Of some pure, forest-broidered stream.
And like the stream, though all unknown
Its voiceless language, yet we know
It murmurs blessings in its flow,

So, without words, I understood
That they were pure of heart, and good.
Contented here I gladly stayed,
And learned full soon their simple speech;
Heard all their legends; saw them place,
With faith that shames who lean on Christ,
Each night a watchman, with his face
Turned to the East, lest He should come—
Great Montezuma—and should find
His people unprepared. They said
That some fair dawn, from out the East,
In robes like flaming fire arrayed,
And on a steed milk-white, and fleet,
That He would come. If not to-night,
Why, then, to-morrow—sometime. He
Had sworn to them, in ages past
That He would come, and they—believed!

They set apart a priestess, too;
Great Montezuma's chosen bride;
The fairest that their nation knew,
And wise, and pure of heart beside.
This one had large and lustrous eyes,
That shone as from some hidden fire;
And hair of purple black, which fell
Down to her waist, with queenly grace.
I sought her out, and touched her heart
By kindly words, until one day,
She drew the veil aside, and lay
Before me all their mysteries.

"Once, long ago," so said the maid,
With her strange eyes that seemed to look

Adown the past, as in a book,
That she, and she alone, could read,
"Once, long ago, there was a time
"When God spake face to face with men,
"And men were pure and unafraid.
"But soon they sinned, and God withdrew
"For countless suns His sacred face;
"He then forgave a chosen few,
"And these the fathers of my race.
"He swore to them that he would send
"His Son, to be an earthly king,
"To rule and bless, till time should end.

"They worshiped Him in many ways;
"By burning beasts; by slaying doves;
"By music, strangely, grandly sweet,
"Of many instruments.   Their feet
"Kept time to holy songs of praise.
"They builded Him a temple grand,
"Where dwelt His priests, in sacred state.
"And all the people, far or near,
"Came up to worship every year.

"And so they lived; until, at length,
"Brother 'gainst brother drew his sword,
"And fought with fierce, unholy strength.
"Our Fathers were defeated.   They
"Then left the land that gave them birth,
"And wandered forth through this wide earth.
"Through blood, and tears, and famine, they,
"For myriad suns, kept on their course.
"And many perished, on the way
"Their swords carved out, with desperate force.

"At length, they conquered this fair land,
"And of their captives chose them wives—
"The rest they slew.   They builded them
"Grand palaces; and chose for king
"Great Montezuma.

                    "All is gone
"Their strength, their greatness, with their lives
"Went out.   And now a feeble band,
"Their children toil from sun to sun,
"Longing for that which is to be.
"With God's own son they now confound
"Great Montezuma.   None but we,
"His priestesses, have kept alive
"The old, old faith.   But He will come,
(How her dark eyes burned mine, like flame!)
"God's glorious Son will surely come
"One day.   What matters then, His name?
"So let them be; they are not wrong
"Who trust in God."
                    With this she turned
To feed a sacred flame, which burned
Less fierce than her mysterious eyes!

Again the spirit of unrest
Returned, and bade me rise, and flee.
I turned tired feet unto the West,
And sought the grand, Pacific sea.
I stood where Colorado cleaves
Great granite mountains sheer in twain.
And, like a monster serpent, weaves
His devious way through desert plains.
I saw the rugged cacti stand,

Stern as some mail-clad sentinel;
I trod the ashen, fevered sands
Of Arizona's desert hell;
I traversed calm and stormy seas;
I stood beneath the pine and palm;
Yet Norland cares, nor tropic ease
Brought not forgetfulness, nor calm.
And in my heart, the whole day long,
Like fairy chime, so soft and clear,
I heard the echo of a song—
"Thou art so far, and yet so near!"

SONG.

I have conned o'er the task thou hast set me
    Again, and again.
I have burned thy sad words, "Forget me!"
    On heart and brain.
Yet, dear love, while memory liveth
    Hope ever will stay;
Unbidden her promise she giveth
    For aye, and for aye!
Oh, stay, then, thy words of rebuke, love,
    Till memory be dead;
And hope, with her visions so sweet, love,
    Forever is fled!

O'er lands and o'er seas I have wandered
    In rest-seeking flight;
With mountains and plains have I sundered
    Thy form from my sight.
Yet the sad waves, with low, ceaseless murmur
    Are crooning thy name;

And in the soft breezes of Summer
  'Tis whispered again.
Oh, pause, then, before chiding me, love,
  For forgetting thy will,
And speak to the winds and the sea, love,
  And bid them be still !

So sad days dawned, in purple and in gold,
In gold and purple did the days expire :
And years (O life from death !) did slow unfold
Out of the mold of their unrealized desire.
And days and years, in vague unrest,
Lapsed by, to make a life unblest.
A life ! How passing strange it is !
How like a song in unknown tongue,
By wandering minstrel sweetly sung,
Of which we hear the quivering notes,
As out upon the air it floats,
But not one word can understand !
We pause, and muse, and wisely guess
What tale the bard would fain convey.
And if the song float clear and strong,
We cry, " Lo, this is triumph's lay !
A song of love, which won its prize ;
A hymn of praise, by victor sung ;
Of hope, for fulfilled prophecies ;
Of bread returned, on waters flung !"
But if the tune die sad away,
" Lo, 'tis a funeral dirge, this lay ;
A tale of piteous distress ;
A wreck, far drifted out from land ;
A woe so hard none understand,
This minstrel's sad, sweet song," we say,

Ah, well ! What is eternity
But years which circle, slow and grand,
Where ere the old comes twice to hand,
'Tis long forgot—and therefore new !
But circling years, though wheeling slow,
Tell out our lives with wondrous speed ;
So let them flit. We can but heed
The summons when it comes—and go !
*　　*　　*　　*　　*　　*

From far-off lands there comes a voice,
"Come back !" O, lost, O, love, rejoice !

POEMS OF HOME.

Many the gifts, and passing fair,
Hath God vouchsafed unto our race;
Yet 'mong'st those that most precious are
Doth memory hold exalted place.
Dear memory, whose silent feet
Become the crutch of halting age,
We tax thee sore and oft; yet sweet
And loving is thy vassalage.
O, nymph, who knows not time nor space,
Link hands and go with me to-day,
For I would wander far away,
And long-abandoned pathways trace.

THE OLD HOMESTEAD.

A FRAGMENT.

'TIS Winter's waning.   Yesterday
    A sleet storm howled the long day through
With stinging fury.   Yet to-day
All is serene and fair to view.
Each tree, encased to utmost twig
Within an icy coat of mail,
Stands like an armored giant, big
With purposes that can not fail.
The clear, cold sun, so far that seems
Yet nearest is of all the year,
Makes the translucent armor gleam
And sparkle like a million spears.
See the still, frozen forest stretch
Its tangled branches leagues away—
Here glittering to the sun's soft touch,
There shaded to a pearly gray.
Above the bare boughs interlace
And frame blue bits of sky between—
No art their beauteous maze can trace,
Nor tongue describe the fairy scene.
Beneath a silence calm, profound,
As though all strife for aye had fled,
Save where with crushing, creaking sound
The snow resents the passer's tread;
Or when, with sound like rifle crack,
A thawing tree fires snapping gun,
While distant echoes answering back,
Show Winter's reign is almost done;

Or when, with earthquake-like report,
A forest monarch, proud and tall,
Judged by some elemental court,
Obeys with sudden, awful fall.

Surprised and timid, here and there,
The white-tailed rabbit leaps away,
With furry foot that treads on air,
So swift he skips and silently ;
And high above, with feet that cling,
The prairie chickens watchful sit,
Ready on whirring, sailing wing,
With quick alarm, away to flit.
Deep in the forest, hid from view,
A river lies, frost-bound and still.
Upon whose breast of glassy hue
An army might encamp at will.
Here drooping willows line its banks,
With boughs caught in its cold embrace ;
Here cottonwoods, in glorious ranks,
Rear high their heads, with stately grace.
And on its banks, within a square
Hewn from the forest's heart, there stands
The farm-house, silvery in the glare
The snow reflects on every hand.
Around its eaves the icicles,
A beauteous cornice, thickly run ;
Stalactites tapering to pearls,
And lengthening in the warming sun.

Near by, with stiff, symmetric grace
The orchard trees rebellious grow,
Each leaning devious from its place,

As if to spoil the hateful row.
A snowy hillock marks the spot
Where last Fall's fruit was stored away,
When pippin, bell-flower, Queen Charlott
In ruddy, golden glory lay,
Till. covered first with clean bright straw,
The earth was heaped with generous hand
So deep that Winter's frost or thaw,
Warm and secure, they could withstand.
And when the brief day's work is done
And the long, cosy evening near,
With eager joy, the children run
To plunder from the treasures here.
The frozen earth is dug away
By fingers numb and red with cold ;
Yet still they burrow carefully
Until the buried fruit they hold.
Then from the loft dry nuts are brought,
And on the grate the wood piled higher,
And snow and cold are set at naught
Before the sparkling, blazing fire.

*   *   *   *   *   *

The time slips by, and April days,
With fickle, chilly showers, are here,
And in the tangled woods a maze
Of swelling, fragrant buds appear.
While waiting not for leafy robes,
The dogwood bursts in sudden bloom ;
And willows, opening tiny lobes,
A fresh and tender green assume.
And in the sheltered, sunny spots

A few wild flowers are nestling found :
Sweet Williams, and Forget-me-nots
Bestar the grass that creeps around.
The smoke curls blue from out the woods
Where dripping fast from cruel wounds,
The maple sap, in generous floods,
Outpours its amber sweets.   Around
The wooden troughs are thickly placed,
And gatherers pass with hasty steps
Lest any overflow.   The taste
With hollow reed to youthful lips
Is sweeter far than ever are
All future draughts that manhood sips.

Afield, the plow glides through the ground
Which last year generous crops returned ;
The earth purrs with a low, soft sound
As each black furrow is upturned.
The musing plowman scarcely heeds
The murmur of the yielding sod :
His soul, attuned to Nature's deeds,
Communes direct with Nature's God.
And feels that since Creation's dawn
The fiat whence all beings springs
Has never ceased.   The very stones
Thrill with the consciousness it brings.
Creation ceases not ; each day,
Each moment feels the eternal force.
And life in myriad, million ways   .
Obeys its sacred, hidden Source.
To live is Nature's Great First Law ;
The base her being rests upon.
And towards some goal, of solemn awe,

Resistlessly life urges on.
Silent, apart, great Nature broods,
With matter plastic in her hands;
And in her countless forms and moods
The finished thought reflected stands.
O, Mother-nature, Mother-god,
We press on towards thy holy shrine!
The form is but the lifeless clod,
The soul, the heart, the purpose thine!

* * * * * *

The woods are now one dense, dark green,
The prairies lose their sullen dun,
And May, robed in her leafy sheen,
Thrills to the kisses of the sun.
Across the field, plowed deep and well,
Light furrows run at equal space,
And to the hasty droppers tell
Where they the golden grain must place.
Behind, with tardier, watchful care,
The coverers bury well the seed.
While blackbirds, circling through the air,
Plan many a wild foraying deed.
So sleep the grains, in darkness wrapped,
Till nature whispers soft, "Increase!"
And breathes her wondrous secret, kept
Locked in her breast in solemn peace.
This Force within the kernel rife
Which thrills, expands, bursts through the sods,
Is the forbidden Tree of Life,
Which, knowing, we shall be as gods!
Then, Nature, guard thy secret well,

For men strive hard, with courage high ;
They press thee close, and who can tell
What hour may bring their triumph nigh ?
What is the flaming sword but sin,
Which blinds our eyes at Eden's gates ?
Lo, purity shall enter in,
Nor fear all adverse gods, nor fates !

*   *   *   *   *   *

The days have passed in patient toil
All through the sunny month of June.
Thrice has the plow stirred fresh the soil
Between green rows, grown tall so soon.
And now July, with fervent heat,
And breathless days that mark its path,
Brings yellow fields of ripened wheat—
The recompense of trust and faith.
"Man can live by faith alone."
Nay ; he each day by faith begins,
And ends by faith, and so atones
Unconsciously his conscious sins.
Each night he yields his soul to sleep—
The mystic prototype of death—
With faith that reason tryst will keep,
And float back on his 'wakening breath.
Through all the devious ways of life
Faith walks before and points the road,
And when we cease the unequal strife,
It leads at last to rest and God.

CULPA MIA.

Two cottages upon the green,
　　Agone, we built us, side by side;
　　And what should brothers' homes divide?
So nothing there we placed between.

A little spark, I know not how,
　　Was fanned into a sudden flame.
　　I thought he wronged me, and there came
Harsh, bitter words between us now.

He could not brook that face to face
　　We stood, in passing out and in;
　　And so our little homes between
At last a cold, high wall did place.

I saw the stones piled up in pride;
　　And I within my heart a wall
　　Higher and prouder built, to pall
The chambers once he occupied.

And then I wandered far away—
　　For half a life we had not met;
　　I thought to find the barrier yet
When I returned, one Summer day.

But, lo! long since it crumbled, fell,
　　And nothing now our homes did part;
　　And suddenly within my heart,
I felt its pride was gone, as well.

Like long-forgotten childhood's rhyme,
　　My brother's voice then softly said,

"Time healeth all,"   With bowéd head,
"Yea," whispered I, "and blessed be time!"

Yet though the needless wound he heals,
    Still there remains the cruel scar
    On hearts and wasted years, to mar
The tear-blurred page the past reveals.

IN THE CHURCHYARD.

THE South wind was laden with dew
    It had kissed from the lips of the clover,
While a faint breath of rose odors, too,
    Betrayed the caress of fond lover,
As the gate op'ed for two to pass through.
    Two hearts that with sorrow were numb
To the graves of their dead were now come
    To live all their grief again over :
And the South wind sighed low and was dumb.

One sought out a monument proud
    Of marble, all sculptured and graven ;
That with cold, lifeless letters avowed
    The tribute affection had given.
But the crushed, bleeding heart there that bowed
    Only saw in the marble a shroud
That barred out all the sweet light of heaven.
    And bitter she wept that the pall
Which had darkened her whole life, should fall
    At the last o'er the tomb it had given.

The other paused by a low mound
    O'er which green, matted grass was fresh growing.

No pile of carved marble was found,
  Either true or false praise vain bestowing;
But daisies and violets fair
  Were nestling contentedly there,
And many a red rose was blowing.
  And the heart of the mourner was glad
When she saw the companions he had
  Were the purest and best earth could bring;
For the loves of the life which has fled
  Now cluster to cheer his lone bed,
And her grief hath no more its sharp sting.

Then the South wind passed on till he came
  To his own trusting sweethearts, the clover;
And the cheek of each bloom was aflame,
  As she tiptoed to kiss her fond lover.
But why such rare, tender caress
  He, lingering, gave none could guess;
But the South wind this thought pondered over:
  There is that which gold never can buy;
Love demands love again, or 'twill die,
  Whether rose-queen or humble, brown clover!
So he stooped with another warm kiss
  For the red lips which reached up to his
So gratefully fond, and from this
  Gave he love to his lowliest lover.

PROMISE.

WHAT though the faded leaves are falling, falling,
   Leaving the gnarled limbs comfortless and bare;
What though the Winter winds are moaning, calling,
   In tones where grief commingles with despair;
Still there remains of Summer days a token,
   A faint, quaint perfume where the flowers have been.
And frowning clouds by sometime rifts are broken
   Through which a hint of Summer warmth drifts in.

What though our souls have failed of high endeavor,
   And grand and noble deeds be all foregone;
What though our tired feet grope onward ever,
   Well knowing that our goal can not be won;
Still purposeful is life, and full of blessing
   Which waits on patient, little deeds of love;
And humble acts, if faith and truth possessing,
   At last a richer recompense may prove.

IN MEMORIAM.

FOR life is like a rosary,
   Which we take up, and, mutt'ring, say
   Its o'erworn beads; then haste away:
   And life hath known its transient day.

And well for us if mayhap we
   E'en its few beads have fully told;
   For feeble is the thread, and old,
   And oft breaks, ere they reach our hold.

Yet thou did'st tell them, one by one :
    Sorrow and grief, and woe, and pain ;
    Peace, rest and heart-balm ; love's sweet bane,
    That slays to make alive again.

Aye, thou did'st learn how passing sweet
    (If bitter sweet, yet how sweet still !)
    Was love, drunk to the very fill,
    Giddy with joy and drowning ill.

The flower that blows to fade at noon,
    The corn, upsprung while frosts still are,
    A song voice, drifting swift afar,
    Heedless of tip-toed listener —

These were thy life.   The sinking sun,
    One-half his rays thrown lovingly
    Toward us, and half as eagerly
    On lands (O, blind !) we can not see,

Such thy sweet death.   Oh, if that we
    Might part the veil that makes us twain
    But one brief moment, how would pain,
    And woe, and heartache—sin's sad train—

Give place and flee !   Life's mystery
    Is death's scroll, closed remorselessly :
    But one alone has read, and he—
  O, Christ-child, lean low now to me !

THE ECHO.

I knew a spot, in olden days,
    Where I have laughed, in childish glee,
    Or sang, or called defiantly,
    And all my words came back to me.

Bytimes I wandered far away;
    The years sped by like wooing time;
    Came flower of youth, came manhood's prime,
    Then came gray hairs, a silvery rime.

And then it chanced I drifted back,
    And found, as wanderers always find,
    All gone that linked me to my kind—
    Not one dear thing was left behind.

Life seemed a troubled dream to me;
    And in my dream I wandered on,
    And as old scenes I mused upon,
    Said sadly to myself, " All gone."

" All gone," returned a low, sad voice.
    I started at the apt reply;
    " Yet you are faithful still," sighed I,
    And " Faithful still," came, with my sigh.

Then, lo! a thing most passing strange,
    The echo's voice died not away
    With mine, as erst it did alway,
    But whispered on, and this did say:

" Men live their little, fleeting hour;
    They strive and war, with eyes afrown;

They fill the earth with their renown—
Sail bold and well, and then go down

"Into the hungry sea of death.
    The world cries out an hour in pain,
    Then turns to war and strive again ;
    And I alone of all remain

"And what am I !   A hollow sound,
    And empty, cruel mockery ;
    Yet all of life is found in me—
    Fit type of unreality !"

THE COUNTRY PARTY.

IN the West, the dying day
    Burned his gold to ashes red,
Blew the ashes with his breath
On the clouds that hung o'erhead.

One by one the stars shone clear,
As we hastened on our way
To the farm house, where that night
Lads and maids from far and near
Met to spend in mirth and play,
Hours that sped wi h hasty flight
On their light-winged, happy way.

Came the lads in groups together,
Came the maids by twos and threes ;
Every lad in se ret fearing
She, of all, might fail to come.

Every lassie wondering whether
He would ask to see her home.
Doubts, like May skies, quickly clearing,
Hers the form he soonest sees,
And the whispered question greets her
In the first nook where he meets her.

Soon the merry games begin
With an "office" full of letters.
Brown-haired lad steps prompt within,
And the dignified postmaster
Duly charged, a lassie calls,
With, "A letter here for you!"
Beats the lassie's pulses faster,
As she steps within to get her
Swift-read, sweet, unwritten letter!
Then to write a fond reply,
Only, strangest of it all,
Not to him who wrote to her
Must she send it. No, indeed;
Other lips must come and read;
Forming thus a circle rare,
For once formed by that same token
Is its power forever broken.
Follow merry forfeits after:
"Heavy, heavy," hanging ever
O'er our heads, but falling never,
For 'mid ringing, joyous laughter,
Oddest penalties are paid
To redeem unlucky "fine,"
While the blushing, coaxing maid
Lighter 'scapes for "superfine."

Then, a most mysterious thing,
Two wise maids declare that they
Own a grand menagerie,
And that we may quickly see
Any animal desired
If we will but blinded be,
And by fair hands captive led.
Every one of course is fired,
And the riddle must be read.
One by one they led us in
With the strictest secrecy ;
Came my turn, and when they asked
What fierce, wild beast they should bring,
For a while my brain I tasked,
Then I called for "baboon straight."
Fell the bandage off my pate,
With a mirror stood an elf,
And I looked and saw—myself !

Followed games in quick succession ;
"Crooked Answer" to "Cross Question,"
"Bridge of Sighs," and then "Surprised ;"
Then two wights we "Mesmerised ;"
"Thimble," "Whistle," "Master Simon ;"
"Hunt the Slipper," "Copenhagen ;"
"Scandal" caused a precious stir ;
Then "Master sent me to you, Sir."
"Proverbs" followed sagely after,
And "Seek the Ring" 'mid ringing laughter.
A "Lawyer" then we interviewed,
And a "Mummy" acted very rude.
A "Prophet" with our fates did chaff ;

And then, to try some nobler thing,
We formed a grave, long-visaged ring,
And had a "Scientific Laugh!"

Ah, how swift the moments fled
With the old folks snug in bed,
And we happy youngsters free
To drink deep love's sweet witchery.
Who so cold as to resist
With red lips pouting to be kissed?
Who so mailed that he withstands
Arrows sped by such fair hands?

Yet whene'er that happy time
Borne on memory's dreamy ships,
Backward drifts, as drifts the rhyme,
Prattled o'er by childish lips,
One swift moment I recall,
Sweetest, dearest of them all,
When before her fathers's door,
Where the stars could only see,
She, my beauteous Eleanore,
Gave one little kiss to me!

TO ———

PERHAPS on earth I'll ne'er again behold,
    With eye of sense, your outward form and semblance,
Therefore, to me, you never will grow old,
    But live, forever young, in my remembrance.

IN SILENCE.

THERE are tears we dare not shed which are bitterer by far,
In their aching, ashen burning, than the freest flowing
are ;
There are griefs we must keep hidden in the chambers of our
heart
That are sharper than all others : bring a keener, deadlier smart.
And the wistful silence waiting on the words we may not say,
In its stillness, holds the fullness of all sorrows on our way.
For the surges of sad dirges half efface the grief they tell,
But the weary woes of silence list in vain a passing knell.

Yet the end is surely coming, and a brighter, fairer dawn
Shall illume the paths of darkness, which our feet now grope
upon.
Not for aye shall grief endure : pain and sorrow will have fled.
"Blessed are the mourners," saith He, "for they shall be
comforted."
And we clasp the promise to us as we float out on the tide,
For we may at least forget when we reach the other side.

BUT THIS.

THE world is full of song
As strong, sweet singers sweep the sounding strings
With chords, fulfilled, of holy, happy things.
I list, and long
But this ; to add one song—
One song as yet unsung, of all the songs they sing.

The world is full of good
As brawny arms do battle for the Right,

And hydra-headed evil ceaseless smite.
        I watch the fray
           With folded arms ; yet sadly pray
But this : to strike one blow, ere fades my transient day.

IN THE GLOAMING.

Now night's purple mantle falleth
    Softly o'er the dying day.
And the wooing twilight calleth
    From the cares of life away.

And we lie contented, dreaming,
    In the restful, tranquil lull,
Painting scenes through fancy gleaming,
    Distant, flitting, beautiful.

Hark ! a song we loved in childoood,
    From afar, floats to our ear.
Bringing meadow, glen and wildwood,
    Drifting on the notes anear.

Peopling silent halls with faces
    That have long slept with the dead,
Yet within our hearts whose places
    Still remain untenanted.

Broken dreams of joy or sorrow,
    Fade before night's thickening ray.
Let us rest, and meet to-morrow
    With the hope born of to-day.

IVY.

Family-laden,
  Wee, wise maiden
Knits her brow in dainty knots.
  How to dolly
  Cure of folly
Occupies her busy thoughts.

  " Dolly's wet her
  Feet, to get her
Posies in the morning dew.
  Sure to be sick—
  Cold or colic ;
Like as not the measles, too !

  "There is Freddy
  Always ready
Into awful 'fairs to fall :
  Bad as Rosy—
  Doodness I
Don't know how to manage, 'tall !

  " Jack or Norah's
  Telled a story !
One or t'uver's ate ma's cake ;
  While there's silly
  Greedy Willy
Got a drefful stomach ache !

  " Naughty Bessie
  Tored her dress ; she
Wants anuver one, I spose ;
  I tell you what,

It takes a lot
Of work to keep my dolls in t'lose !

Look, she lays her
Down by Cæsar—
What can be the matter now ?
Blue eyes closing,
Winking, dozing,
Wee, white hands and lily brow—

Cheeks so waxen.
Tresses flaxen,
Footstep, that a fairy's seems—
All now wander
Over yonder,
In the happy land of dreams !

CONTENTMENT.

THERE is an island hidden far
    Beyond the gray horizon's rim
And sometimes wandering ships there are
    Who see its shores rise, white and dim.

And some have turned them from their way,
    With wistful eyes, and sailed anigh ;
And looked and longed a Summer's day—
    Then passed the isle forever by.

Of these, some said, on grassy banks
    Stood palaces, all white and fair ;
And tropic trees, in stately ranks,
    And gold, and precious stones were there.

And others said : Not so ; the isle
  Resounds but to the trump of fame,
Where legions strive for fortune's smile,
  And honor's death-surviving name.

And others, weary-eyed, did see
  Fair homes, where wives and children were;
Said others : There green woodlands be,
  Afar from every haunt of care.

And each sighed : Oh, that I might cast
  My anchor in its coral bays !
My life would be fulfilled at last,
  And peace be mine, through all my days !

But some there were who from the rest
  Stood sad apart, and silently ;
Yet questioned close, at last confessed
  That they had touched its shores, one day.

" A cruel mirage," whispered these,
  " Where many a vision fair is shown ;
But all who reach its bowers of ease
  Find burning wastes of sand alone ! "

EL CABO DE TODOS.

U NDER the pines where the zephyrs blew by
    Filled with faint fragrance of sweet-smelling gum,
And odors of delicate flowers anigh,
  He stood, and dreamed of the days to come.
Fair as the isles of Hesperides
  A future of wealth and fame upsprung ;

And o'er and o'er, like a pulse of the seas,
　　His heart beat loud, "I am young; I am young!"

Under an oak, in the Summer heat,
　　With a bird glancing down, with a side-turned head,
And the breeze filled with perfume of maize and wheat,
　　He stood, and mused o'er the years that had fled.
His dreams of wealth had faded away,
　　And fame had passed by, like a street-caroled song;
Yet fairer than they seemed contentment to-day,
　　And his heart beat firm, "I am strong; I am strong!"

Under the willow, whose quivering leaves
　　Tremble and shake, like an old man's hands,
Where the only odor the wind receives
　　Is the earthy scent of the fallowed lands,
He stands, and mumbles a broken thread
　　Of words, as rosary beads are told;
His dreams, unrealized, all are dead,
　　And his heart feebly beats, "I am old; I am old!"

ARMAGEDDON.

Lo, EARTH is portentious with omens,
　　And the skies answer back with a frown;
Men whisper distrustful; and no man
　　　　Secure lieth down.

For the mutter of gathering legions
　　Is heard from mountain to sea;
Near at hand, and from far-away regions—
　　　　Wherever men be.

DRIFTINGS IN DREAMLAND.

Not for battles of czars, kings or princes,
  Where brother 'gainst brother is led,
But the desperate fight for existence—
      The struggle for bread !

For the lordlings and rich scourge and flay us,
  And squander the fruits of our toil ;
And our rulers despise and betray us,
  And bind us for spoil.

Our teachers corrupt and delude us ;
  Our counselors lead us astray ;
Our law-makers strip and denude us ;
      Our priests—what are they ?

Their souls, lean with longings and famine,
  They cry up, and offer for sale ;
They are bought with the lucre of Mammon,
      They are prophets of Baal !

UNRECOGNIZED.

'NEATH banyan tree, in Afric lands,
      A traveller rested from the heat.
Half buried in the burning sands,
  A pebble sparkled at his feet.
He picked it up, and toyed with it ;
  Tossed it aloft, in idle play,
Then in a dreamy, absent fit,
  He careless threw it far away.
He who had roamed o'er every land,
  With thirst for gold his only guide,

When it lay fair within his hand,
  The wealth of Ind had flung aside !

Within her bower a maiden fair
  Lay, dreaming of a love to be ;
 A love as pure as lilies are,
   As constant as the changeless sea.
And while she dreamed, that summer morn,
  A lover came and knelt to her ;
She laughed his humble suit to scorn,
  And banished thus her worshiper.
She who but dreamed as poets do
  Of love alone, the live-long day,
Now failed to recognize the true,
  And cast her whole life's love away !

O, blind, blind Fate, thou leadest men
  By ways too hard to understand !
Thy mysteries we cannot ken,
  Nor loose the grip of thy strong hand.
O, goddess cruel, goddess blind !
  Thou who hast led us all our days,
Art sure that thou the way canst find,
  That lies beyond life's tangled maze ?
See, thou hast wrecked full many a ship
  By steering where wild waves o'erwhelm ;
Oh, loosen, then, thy fatal grip
  And to our hands resign the helm !

YOUTHFUL POEMS.

POSSESSION.

Thou art mine own, O love! Thy heart
    Beats time to mine, with throbbings sweet
    And musical as coming feet
Of loved ones, after years apart.

Thou art mine own, O sweet! Thy lips
    Melt into mine, with kisses rare
    As Arab's magic balm, that slips
Straight to the heart, to banish care.

Thou are mine own, O fond! Thy head
    Resting so lightly on my breast
    Brings dreams as rare as ever sped
To bless a wanderer's toil-won rest.

IN GOLDEN GATE PARK.

Nay, do not turn away your head,
    Love; I must speak, and you shall hear!
    Here, 'midst this faint, sweet perfume, dear,
I cannot leave one word unsaid.

Will you still stand, with drooping lid,
    And lips, where frowns such pretty pout?
    Nay, I will kiss their shadow out;
See, we are flower-engulfed, and hid!

For if you wished that I should go
    With all my love sealed in my heart—
    A tomb grass-grown, unknown, apart—
You had not brought me here, I know.

For this is love's own dream of love,
    Voiced into life; these splendid banks,
    So starry-hued, are serried ranks
Of votaries his truth that prove !

And here, amid the pines and firs,
    'Neath drooping fuschias, all aflame
    With love's delicious, tender shame,
And incense on each breath that stirs

Of roses, and of mignonette,
    Of larkspurs, ranged with martial pride,
    In purple hoods, the way beside,
And of the blue-eyed violet,

Love, I must speak, or faint and die !
    For I have loved you, loved you so,
    With love as pure as is the snow
Of these white lilies, sailing by.

(O, breath of balmy, tropic air,
    O, maze of plantain and of palm,
    O, sleeping ferns, your wondrous calm
Is as a spirit's, freed from care !)

(O, birds, that warble tuneful lays,
    O, gold-fish, swimming soft below,
    Your lives are dreams of love, I know,
And peace, and joy haunt all your days !)

And here 'mid beauty's regal reign,
 Where this fair Park, sea-girt, yet free,
 Reaches white fingers to the sea,
Which leans and yearns to her again.

Sweet, you shall surely answer! Hark!
 O, voice, low-tuned to lover's ear,
 "I cannot say thee nay here, dear!"
Now, heaven bless the Golden Park!

A PICTURE.

COME, sit you here, and I will paint
 Your picture, fair and true, for you.
For poets must be painters, too;
And some are grand ones; some are quaint;
And many paint so strangly true.

Yes, you are beautiful.   A brow
As white as snow white lilies are;
And large, blue eyes, enshaded now,
Now gazing absently afar;
A mouth so like a rose-bud, ripe
From sun kiss and the rain s warm love;
A face of Greece's oval type
From pointed chin to brow above;
A swan-like neck; a sylph-like form;
A skin as satin soft and warm—
All, all are beautiful; but, hold!
(A painter close and hard must look,)
That snow-white brow as snow is cold,
And selfish lines, as in a book,

Are written there; and in your eyes
There is a cunning, inward look,
As though in men you had no faith,
But met their lies with other lies
Which sweeter were to you than truth!
O those hard eyes—how plain are writ
Lines which no man can e'er mistake!
Your love, a feeble reed, will break
And pierce him through who leans on it.
For like a vane, with fickle whim,
You veer to every passing breeze.
Your'God is Self, and e'en in him
You put no trust nor faith, Louise.

And I have loved you.   I who bring
The deep love of a child of song;
For to the throng of those who sing
By many a tie I do belong.
By birthright; by the blood that runs
From Scotia's hills, in fiery strains,
And heated hot 'neath Southland suns
Leaps fast and dizzy through my veins;
By that baptismal font of fire
Where Sorrow consecrates her own,
When, faint from unattained desire,
They kneel low at her sable throne;
By that proud will of those who dare
To look on that Throne's dazzling light
And question Him who sitteth there
If earth is ruled by Wrong or Right;
By each of these, by more than these,
I know well what I am.   Alas!

You are so far beneath, Louise,
And I have loved you : let it pass.

No mantle old of prophecy
Upon my shoulders needs to fall,
No wierd, strange gift of minstrelsy
To aid my ken have I to call,
To read the fate that waits for you
As waits the dead the funeral pall.
While beauty s flame is yet alight
Weak moths will circle near its glare,
But when that light is set in night,
How dark will be your deep despair !
How you will learn with bitter moan
That man just claims has upon man,
And who live for themselves alone
Must die alone, as best they can !
When you are loveless, friendless, old,
Will you look back and long for these ?
It may be not ; you are so cold
You may not care at all, Louise !

RETRIBUTION.

SOFTLY the moonmist fell down and enshrouded you,
Wrapped you around with its silvery light.
Passionless, cold as the beams that beclouded you,
Turned you away from my pleading that night—
Turned my day into night !

I who from sorrow's dark portals had fled to you,
Fled at your call, as a moth to the light.

Hung'ring for love's long-delayed feast, I sped to you,
  Sped as the blind sped of old for their sight—
      To the Master for sight.

Then for a time, like a pleased child, you toyed with me —
  Filling my soul with a maddening delight ;
Not for a moment I dreamed you were cloyed with me,
  Not till the moonrays enrobed you that night
      With their cold, loveless light.

Wounded to death, then I turned me away from you,
  Turned as the Lost turn from heaven's sweet light.
Bitter as seemed it forever to stay from you,
  Bitterer far to remain in your sight,
      In your cold, cruel sight.

So.   As one walks among tombs am I wandering,
  Plucking Dead Sea fruit from morn until night.
Daily my birthright for pottage am squandering,
      For the blighted must blight.

And you—Life is naught but a ripple of song to you,
  Lover moths, fresh, are e'er seeking your light.
Yet sometime ! I envy not thoughts which must throng to you
  When the tide turns and life ebbs into night—
      Black, desolate night.

AFTER CHURCH.

Where a tiny path
  Threaded through the heather,
Lizzie walked with me—
  Very close together.

Bluebells nodded wisely
  To the daisies, lowly,
As they watched us, going
  Home so slowly, slowly.
Aye; they nodded, nodded,
  Till their heads were dizzy,
Did they know she loved me,
  Witching, winsome Lizzie?
Yet I durst not ask them—
  She had heard me, surely;
Maiden at my side,
  Walking so demurely.
So we passed along
  Through the feathery heather,
Talking of the fashions,
  Talking of the weather.
Saying naught of loving,
  Though my thoughts were busy
Conning something over
  I must tell to Lizzie,
When we reached the gate,
  Suddenly bold-hearted,
Plead I for a kiss—
  Just one—ere we parted.
O'er her swept a thrill—
  Would she chide, resist me?
Sudden, while I doubted,
  Tiptoed she, and kissed me!

Kissed, and ran away
  Both ere scarce I knew it,
Fond, yet half in terror
  That she e'er should do it.

And I walked blithe back,
  With the daisies wond'ring
Why I seemed so happy
  O'er such sudden sund'ring.
But a saucy bluebird
  Stoutly did insist him—
Chirruped loud, "I know,
  Lizzie kissed him, kissed him!"

WINONA.

A SHIMMER of star glints; a heaven of amber,
    Arching the brilliants of God's diadem;
Dim outlines of meadows whose uncertain shadows
  Change and shift, as we gaze, like an opaline gem.

A song in the wind, as of far-away singer
  Low voicing a joy that will not be controlled;
A hinting of perfumes, that loiter and linger;
  A dream that links heaven and earth in its hold.

For she stood beside me, while, breeze-blown and lightly,
  Her curls tossed and rippled against my fond breast;
As with pretty rebellion, so faintly, so lightly,
  The beautiful head fluttered down to its rest.

Then the stars drifted up from the East, and then over;
  And the meadows grew gray wastes of shadowy swells;
And the song in the wind, as it swept o'er the clover,
  Changed into the clamor of glad wedding bells.

A DREAM OF THE TROPICS.

Fret of surf, which ceaseth never
      From its moaning, soft and low;
Lap of tides, which ever, ever
      Come and go, come and go;
Emerald-vestured shores of coral,
      Broidered rich with golden beams;
Forests dumb, or only oral
      With the voiceless tones of dreams;
Lo! with slow steps, doubting taken,
      To your peaceful shrines I come.
Let me not your dreams awaken;
      I am dumb; I am dumb.

Strange, rare songsters flit before me,
      Noiseless as the shadows creep,
And, in star-crowned palm trees o'er me,
      Leaf-hid, sit in dreamless sleep;
Dew-kissed, incense-breathing flowers
      Scatter perfume as I tread;
Wild, blue creepers twine o'er bowers
      With white lilies carpeted;
Cockatoos, rare green and golden,
      Climbing, swing by amber beak;
Or, among the branches olden,
      Hide and seek; hide and seek.

At my feet the gray Iguanas
      Startled, ope dim eyes of pearls,
Glide and hide where dense bananas
      Thrust their crowding, clustering whorls;
Oranges, gold-dusted, yellow,

Tempt me with their fruitage sweet;
Drooping plantains, creamy, mellow,
  Whisper, " Eat ; take and eat ! "
Palms with milk-full cocoas laden,
  Drop their nuts with rustling clink ;
Saying, "'Toil not; here is Aidenn ;
  Take and drink ; take and drink ! "

'Mid the pure white lily ocean,
  Lovely, brown-skinned maidens move ;
Every graceful, sylph-like motion
  Breathing, " Love ; look, and love ! "
Voices soft as echo, calling
  O'er and o'er its low replies ;
Warm, round bosoms, rising, falling,
  With love s rapt, delighted sighs ;
Soul-pure dreamers, knowing never
  Blush of shame or sting of sin,
Dream on ; dream sweet dreams forever ;
  Only pause and dream me in !

UNREST.

OH, the weary, weary yearning burning through my heart
    and brain !
Beat my pulses dirge-like throbbings, sobbings of a stifled pain ;
For my love is still delaying, staying all these empty years.
Though I've waited patient, trusting, thrusting back hot, un-
    wept tears.

Fades the Spring to Summer weary, dreary comes brown Au-
    tumn then ;
Bitter winds of Winter blow, and lo ! the Spring is here again

Bringing only with its coming, humming of a far-off song—
Love-song of a maiden saintly, faintly borne the breeze along.

Bloom the roses in the valleys, dallies each with lover fond ;
Stoops the breeze to kiss the lily, stilly nestling on the pond ;
Every dove his love is wooing, cooing o'er the building nest,
And the robin's notes are trilling, thrilling through his mate's
    fond breast.

Only I am lorn and lonely, only I am desolate ;
Hasten, then, long-tarrying maiden, laden with my song of
    fate.
Hasten for the years are hasting, wasting like the snows of
    June—
Come, and still my life's harsh discords and my soul with
    thine attune !

SONNET.—ACROSTIC.

To FEEL that life is sweet ; to hear
    One endless song the long day through,
Low toned and soft, as when from far,
O'er moonlit waters, deep and blue,
Vespers of eve float to the ear,
Encentring joys of pregnant years
In one sharp hour of present bliss
Sweet as an age of heaven is !
To love till life, and love grow one—
Oh, this is life, and only this.
Life which before was barren grain
Impregnate is by love's warm sun ;
Vaticinal it shall remain
E'en till eternal life is done !

A BURIAL HYMN.

DEAD.   Let the days as with Autumn leaves cover it;
　　Days blown like leaves from the great tree of Time.
Bid the light breezes to chant dirges over it ;
　　Bid frosts to enshroud it with delicate rime.

Dead.   Will it ever be covered, be hidden,
　　This love, o'er which dead days are sighing and falling ?
Will the sharp gusts of memory, unwelcome, unbidden,
　　For aye lift the pall, with such cruel recalling ?

Dead.   Do dull dirges drown doubt's dumb despairing
　　When, heart-faint and hopeless, we bury our dead ?
Shall I ever forget ?   Shall I sometime cease caring ?
　　Oh, answer, yeleaves that I crush with my tread !

ADIÓS.

"TO GOD."   The Spaniard's soft good bye
　　Seems fittest for the parting word,
The sad, sad word, which must be heard
While men shall live and love, and die.
We dreamed the old, old dream a time ;
We heard the old, old wooing song ;
The hours we weaved in happy rhyme,
And days were years, and years were long,
And full of joy as clinging kiss
Which meed of faithful waiting is !

"To God."   For us the sounding sea
Shall make no more sweet melody.

No more its waves drune soothing songs,
Nor proud ships float its tides along;
No more shall birds sing soft; no more
Fair flowers spring our paths before.

Ah, well! What other dreams we dream,
Still strangely sweet will this one seem—
This one dead dream, which now we lay
So deep within its grave away.

May roses bloom above the sod,
And thou—O, lost, my love, "To God!"

IN AN ALBUM.

THIS experience has taught me; that we on the beach
  Of friendship's wide ocean our names are e'er tracing,
Nor heed that time's tide, in its next hungry reach,
  As fast as we write our fond words is effacing.

Yet sometimes the sands change to stone, and the trace
  Remains firm and clear throughout ages and ages.
So affection's fond lines time can never efface
  Though Death lay his hand on the heart's folded pages.

IN RETROSPECT.

O, SOUL, I speak you fair to-night,
  As one would with a brother speak,
For I am faint of heart, and weak,
And cannot see my way aright.

When I am weak, thou must be strong,
And take the helm with steady hand,
For we have sailed together long,
And both must sink, or both make land !
O'er what strange seas have we not roamed,
What fierce storms we have weathered through,
What fair, green isles dawned to our view,
What bleak, bare coasts a-lee have loomed !

Yet would not I, if I might choose
To trace the same track out again,
Or still drift on an unknown main,
The unknown for the known refuse.
No ; life has not been good to me—
Nor yet has it been over bad.
The joys and griefs which it has had
Have fallen not unequally.
If sorrow's waves have o'er me rolled,
So pleasures, too, have filled my sail
With perfumed winds, from forests old
As time, and dripping, like white hail,
Their fragrant gums.   Then will not I
Lift hand, nor make complaining cry
E'en tho' I sink o'erwhelmed and die.

For life unchastened yet by woe,
By sorrow unbaptized, and grief,
Not yet is life.   We cannot know—
Nay, to the deepest springs of life
Pale sorrow shows alone the way.
And whom she farthest leads are they
Who best know why this fitful gleam

Of consciousness, this passing dream
Is given us; who penetrate
Somewhat the gloom enshrouding fate—
In her dark rites Initiate!

DRIFT WITH THE TIDE.

WHEREFORE should we pull weary oar
    Against the tide that bears us on,
When, of the shores that lie before,
We know not which we'll drift upon?
For aught we know our boats will go,
Straight steered, if slow, to fairy seas,
Where tropic trees give to the breeze
Sweet perfume, as with dreamy ease
We glide by isles where Summer smiles,
And joy beguiles forevermore.

Nay, looking back along our track
Or bright or black, through life's wide sea,
Have our own hands held fast the helm?
Are we now where we thought to be?
Some steered for Pleasure's rose-strewn shores,
Some sailed for Duty's rock-bound coast;
For greed or gain some pulled strong oars,
And some sought storms—glad to be lost.
Yet these the waves would not o'erwhelm,
And those, who have not gone awreck, ·
Drift wide their hopes, at fate's sterm beck.

One unshipped oars and set a sail,
And said, "Let North or South winds blow,

My boat shall sail before the gale;
And where it blows, there will I go."
Lo! fairies shaped each envious breeze
To guide that helmless boat aright;
It drifted straight to dreamy seas,
Shored in by lands of strange delight.
Oh, when before may lie such shore,
Wherefore, O tired, pull weary oar?"

MADONNA MIA.

O, THE love of loving woman!
    Who can tell,
Who can measure or compute
All the heights and depths it reaches,
All the paths its rays illumine!

How like reaching, clinging tendril
Of the vine,
Silently and softly twining,
Hiding 'neath its leafy veil
Where our rugged natures fail.
And the wine
Of its crushed and bleeding fruit
How it floweth red, and goeth
Straightway to our thirsty hearts,
Warming, thrilling in its filling!
Sin may mar it,
Yet it sits a desolate queen—
Sits a pale, mute Magdalene,
Ready, swift at mercy's call

To atone its awful fall.
Not the chill of prison bars,
Not the taint of crime or shame,
Tho' the world's fierce howling jars,
Can obscure or dim its flame.

Let it burn !
In its strength we faintly see
Type of that unfathomed love
Which above
Holds within its boundless sea
Promise of eternity !

EVENING AND MORNING.

LAST night the sun sank red ; the sky,
   Purpled and mottled as with human gore,
Frowned back his lurid glances ; saw him die,
And bade him bitter speed, and I—
   I cried, "O, sun, sink now for aye ; wake me to pain no
     more !"

This morn he rose, with brilliant hues,
   And nature—all forgotten last eve's mood—
Greeted him gladly ; did not e'en refuse
Her rosiest kisses. How could I but choose
   To heed the lesson ; to forget past woes in present good !

FICKLE SORROW.

ONCE a fairy called Hope, came and dwelt in my heart,
    And cheerily sang all one long Winter's day;
And, softly I said, "Thou wilt never depart,
    For love with his charms shall compel thee to stay."
        So I built her a throne,
        And crowned her a queen;
        And a fairer, I ween,
        Than mine was there none.

But the morning brought Spring, with its buds and its flowers,
    And my Hope grew aweary of crown and of throne;
And longed for new kingdoms, new blossoms, new bowers,
    And ever sighed, plaintive, "Oh, let me be gone!"
        But I answered her Nay;
        And bade Love forge a chain
        She might not snap in twain,
        And so bound her for aye.

Then I called Love, and said: "Be thou keeper, and see
    That our captive has all heart can ask;
None can teach her but thou not too long to be free,
    So do thou, gentle Love, take this task.
        Alas, I know not
        How cruel Love is!
        How he slays with a kiss
        When that kiss is unsought!

And so, ere I dreamed it, my sweet Hope was dead;
    And gently I loosened the chain,
That but bound a pale corse, whose spirit had fled
    Forever from me, and her pain.

So I built her a tomb
In my heart, leal and true;
Shut out from my view,
Shut in by deep gloom.

Then Sorrow I charged with its keeping, and said:
  "See. I wander for rest far away;
Keep sacred this chamber where lieth my dead
  Till the time of my coming, I pray."
          Then the moments flew by
          Till a year had been told;
          And the world seemed less cold;
          Less dark the blue sky.

Then Sorrow I called, and again sought the gloom
  Of my tomb.   Lo, no tomb was there!
Only warbling of song-birds and roses in bloom,
  And perfume and joy in the air!
          Not a stone marked my dead;
          And I turned fierce around
          To chide Sorrow, and found
          That she, too, had fled!

A FRAGMENT.

"And I am old, and life for me
      Has naught of love nor hope nor joy?"
Nay; ne'er were years so fair, so free
    From all that love and hope destroy.

For when I ceased to strive and war,
    Lo! life no more flung bloody gage;

But bade me lift mine eyes afar
   And view my glorious heritage.

The joy that shines in her pure eyes
   Whose marriage morn her lover brings;
Of her who bends her, tenderwise,
   And o'er her first born softly sings;

The thrill of those who hear once more
   The echoes of the hastening tread,
When frozen deep or coral shore
   Reluctant yield those mourned as dead—

All, all are mine ! I hear the songs
   Of lovers who have their own have won;
Glad pæans over righted wrongs;
   Soft dirges o'er a fallen one.

And so I sit, with folded hands,
   Contented, on life's utmost shore;
I see the loom of shining lands,
   I wait the boat that bears me o'er.

And, waiting, turn with tender care,
   Life's leaves, grown yellow now and dim.
On every page fair records are
   Of love to me and mine from Him.

There is no grief. Lo, unbelief
   May wince beneath the chastening rod;
But faith beneath the trial brief
   Discerns the upward path to God.

There is no pain.   Lo, life again
  Takes up the burden of its song,
And faith and hope and trust remain
  To light the soul its way along.

A MEMORY.

A SMALL white hand, whose timid touch
    Conceals so much, reveals so much ;
A face lit with the tender pride
Of not one wish unsatisfied ;
And silence that is musical
With worrdless songs—and that is all !

All.   Yet our lives may ebb and flow,
And loves may come and loves may go,
Nor life, nor love again confess
A moment of such perfectness.
Life may be long, and love abide,
Yet neither wholly satisfied.

Ah, well !   All this is past, I wean,
And harsh thoughts interpose between.
Yet nought can ever have the power
To dim the memory of that hour—
That hour so full of all life brings
To hush our yearning questionings.

And when there comes the unbidden thought
Of you, all else shall be forgot ;
And I will paint you with the grace
Of that dear hour upon your face ;
A grace too perfect to abide,
Of love fulfilled and satisfied !

An Epitome of Theosophy.

Theosophy, the Wisdom-Religion, has existed from immemorial time. It offers us a theory of nature and of life which is founded upon knowledge acquired by the Sages of the past, more especially those of the East ; and its higher students claim that this knowledge is not something imagined or inferred, but that it is seen and known by those who are willing to comply with the conditions. Some of its fundamental propositions are :

1.—That the spirit in man is the only real and permanent part of his being ; the rest of his nature being variously compounded, and decay being incident to all composite things, everything in man but his spirit is impermanent.

   Further, that the universe being one thing and not diverse, and everything within it being connected with the whole and with every other, of which upon the upper plane, above referred to, there is a perfect knowledge, no act or thought occurs without each portion of the great whole perceiving and noting it. Hence all are inseparably bound together by the tie of Brotherhood

2.—That below the spirit and above the intellect is a plane of consciousness in which experiences are noted, commonly called man's "spiritual nature": this is as susceptible of culture as his body or his intellect.

3.—That this spiritual culture is only attainable as the grosser interests, passions, and demands of the flesh are subordinated to the interests, aspirations, and needs of the higher nature ; and that this is a matter of both system and established law

4.—That men thus systematically trained attain to clear insight into the immaterial, spiritual world, their interior faculties apprehending Truth as immediately and readily as physical faculties grasp the things of sense, or mental faculties those of reason ; and hence that their testimony to such Truth is as trustworthy as is that of scientists or philosophers to truth in their respective fields.

5.—That in the course of this spiritual training such men acquire perception of and control over various forces in Nature unknown to others, and thus are able to perform works usually called "miraculous," though really but the result of larger knowledge of natural law.

6.—That their testimony as to super-sensuous truth, verified by their possession of such powers, challenges candid examination from every religious mind.

Turning now to the system expounded by these Sages, we find as its main points :—

1.—An account of cosmogony, the past and future of this earth and other planets; the evolution of life through mineral, vegetable, animal and human forms.

2.—That the affairs of this world and its people are subject to cyclic laws, and that during any one cycle the rate or quality of progress appertaining to a different cycle is not possible.

3.—The existence of a universally diffused and highly ethereal medium, called the "Astral Light" or "Akasa," which is the repository of all past, present and future events, and which records the effects of spiritual causes and of all acts and thoughts from the direction of either spirit or matter. It may be called the Book of the Recording Angel.

4.—The origin, history, development and destiny of mankind.

Upon the subject of *Man* it teaches:—

1.—That each spirit is a manifestation of the One Spirit, and thus a part of all. It passes through a series of experiences on incarnation, and is destined to ultimate re-union with the Divine.

2.—That this incarnation is not single but repeated, each individuality becoming re-embodied during numerous existences in successive races and planets, and accumulating the experiences of each incarnation towards its perfection.

3.—That between adjacent incarnations, after grosser elements are first purged away, comes a period of comparative rest and refreshment, the spirit being therein prepared for its next advent into material life.

4.—That the nature of each incarnation depends upon the merit and demerit of the previous life or lives, upon the way in which the man has lived and *thought;* and that this law is inflexible and wholly just.

5.—That "Karma,"—a term signifying two things, the law of ethical causation (Whatsoever a man soweth, that shall he also reap,) and the balance or excess of merit or demerit in any individual, determines also the main experiences of joy and sorrow in each incarnation, so that what men call "luck" is in reality "desert",—desert acquired in past existence.

6.—That the process of evolution up to re-union with the Divine contemplates successive elevations from rank to rank of power and usefulness, the most exalted beings still in the flesh being known as Sages, Rishees, Brothers, Masters, their great function being the preservation at all times, and, when cyclic laws permit, the extension, of spiritual knowledge and influence among humanity.

7.—That when union with the Divine is effected, all the events and experiences of each incarnation are known.

As to the *process* of spiritual development it teaches:—

1:—That the essence of the process lies in the securing of supremacy to the highest, the spiritual, element of man's nature.

2.—That this is attained along four lines, among others,—

(a) The eradication of selfishness, in all forms, and the cultivation of broad, generous sympathy in and effort for the good of others.

(b) The cultivation of the inner, spiritual man by meditation, communion with the Divine, and exercise.

(c) The control of fleshly appetites and desires; alllower, material interests being deliberately subordinated to the behests of the spirit.

(d) The careful performance of every duty belonging to one's station in life, without desire for reward, leaving results to Divine law.

3.—That while the above is incumbent on and practicable by all religiously-disposed men, a yet higher plane of spiritual attainment is conditioned upon a specific course of training physical, intellectual and spiritual, by which the internal faculties are first aroused and then developed.

4.—That an extension of this process is reached in Adeptship, an exalted stage attained by laborious self-discipline and hardship, protracted through possibly many incarnations, and with many degrees of initiation and preferment, beyond which are yet other stages ever approaching the Divine.

As to the *rationale* of spiritual development it asserts:—

1.—That the process is entirely *within* the individual himself, the motive, the effort, the result being distinctly personal.

2.—That, however personal and interior, this process is not unaided, being possible, in fact, only through close communion with the Supreme Source of all strength.

As to the *degree* of advancement in incarnations it holds:—

1.—That even a mere intellectual acquaintance with Theosophic truth has great value in fitting the individual for a step upwards in his next earth-life, as it gives an impulse in that direction.

2.—That still more is gained by a career of duty, piety and beneficence.

3.—That a still greater advance is attained by the attentive and devoted use of the means to spiritual culture heretofore stated.

It may be added that Theosophy is the only system of religion and philosophy which gives a satisfactory explanation of such problems as these:

1.—The object, use, and inhabitation of other planets than this earth.

2.—The geological cataclysms of earth; the frequent absence of intermediate types in its fauna; the occurrence of architectural and other relics of races now lost, and as to which ordinary science has nothing but vain conjecture; the nature of extinct civilizations and the causes of their extinction; the persistence of savagery and the unequal development of existing civilization; the differences, physical and internal, between the various races of men; the line of future development.

3.—The contrasts and unisons of the world's faiths, and the common foundation underlying them all.

4.—The existence of evil, of suffering, and of sorrow—a hopeless puzzle to the mere philanthropist or theologian.

5.—The inequalities in social condition and privilege ; the sharp contrasts between wealth and poverty, intelligence and stupidity, culture and ignorance, virtue and vileness ; the appearance of men of genius in families destitute of it, as well as other facts in conflict with the law of heredity ; the frequent cases of unfitness of environment around individuals, so sore as to embitter disposition, hamper aspiration and paralyze endeavor ; the violent antithesis between character and condition ; the occurrence of accident, misfortune, and untimely death—all of them problems solvable only by either the conventional theory of Divine caprice or the Theosophic doctrines of Karma and Reincarnation.

6.—The possession by individuals of psychic powers—clairvoyance, clairaudience, etc., as well as the phenomena of psychometry and statuvolism.

7.—The true nature of genuine phenomena in spiritualism, and the proper antidote to superstition and to exaggerated expectation.

8.—The failure of conventional religions to greatly extend their areas, reform abuses, re-organize society, expand the idea of brotherhood, abate discontent, diminish crime, and elevate humanity ; and an apparent inadequacy to realize in individual lives the ideal they professedly uphold.

1.—That of intellectual inquiry—to be met by works in Public Libraries, etc.

2.—That of desire for personal culture—to be met partly by the books prepared for that specific end, partly by the periodical Magazines expounding Theosophy.

3—That of personal identification with the Theosophical Society, an association formed in 1875 with three aims—to be the nucleus of a Universal Brotherhood ; to promote the study of Aryan and other Eastern literatures, religions and sciences ; to investigate unexplained laws of nature and the psychical powers latent in man. Adhesion to the first only is a prerequisite to membership, the others being optional. The Society represents no particular creed, is entirely unsectarian, and includes professors of all faiths, only exacting from each member that toleration of the beliefs of others which he desires them to exhibit towards his own.

Membership in the Theosophical Society may be either " at large" or in a local Branch. Applications for membership in a Branch should be addressed to the local President or Secretary ; those " at large" to any Branch President or to the General Secretary, Wm. Q. Judge, 144 Madison Ave., New York, and the latter should inclose $2.00 for entrance fee and 50 cents for diploma, and $1.00 yearly dues. Information as to organization and other points may also be obtained from Secretary Pacific Coast Corporation, Mercantile Library Building, San Francisco.

There are now, 1894, one hundred Branches in the United States, including all the principal cities, among which may be noted New York, Philadelphia, Chicago, St. Louis, San Francisco, Los Angeles, Minneapolis, Washington, Cincinnati, Boston, Omaha, San Diego, Denver, Salt Lake, New Orleans, etc.

REINCARNATION.

A STUDY OF THE, HUMAN SOUL

In its Relation to Re-Birth, Evolution, Post-Mortem
States, the Compound Nature of Man,
Hypnotism, Etc.

BY JEROME A. ANDERSON, M. D., F. T. S.

CONTENTS.

THEOSOPHY.

☞ The Pacific Coast Committee for Theosophic work has opened a Repository of Books at the Theosophical Headquarters, Mercantile Library Building, San Francisco.

Experience indicates the following as a good series of books in a preliminary course :

What is Theosophy? Besant-Olds	$ .35
Short Glossary of Theosophical Terms,	
" " cloth, 75c ; paper	.50
Theosophy and its Evidences, A. Besant,	.10
Wilkesbarre Letters on Theosophy, Alex. Fullerton	.10
Echoes from the Orient, W. Q. Judge	.50
Ocean of Theosophy, W. Q. Judge	1.00
Seven Principles of Man, Annie Besant	.35
Reincarnation, Dr. J. A. Anderson,	1.00
Death and After, Annie Besant	.35
Reincarnation, Annie Besant	.35
Letters that Have Helped Me, Jasper Neimand	.50
Voice of the Silence, H. P. Blavatsky	.75
Bhagavad Gita (pocket edition, morocco), W. Q. Judge	1.00
Esoteric Buddhism, A. P. Sinnett	1.00
The Key to Theosophy, H. P. Blavatsky	1.50
Isis Unveiled, 2 vols	7.50
The Secret Doctrine, 2 vols	10.50

In addition to the above the following is a partial list of books which will also be sent post-paid on receipt of price. Complete lists, including many leaflets and cheap but very useful tracts, papers by Oriental Pundits, sent on application:—

Addresses at American Convention, Chicago, April, 1892	.20
Adventure Among the Rosicrucians, F. Hartman....cloth, 75c; paper,	.50
Astral Light, Nizida	.75
A Rough Outline of Theosophy, Besant	.10
A Study of Man, Dr. J. D. Buck	2.50
Bhagavad Gita, Mohini's Translation and Notes	2.00
Burial Service	.50
Buddhism, Rhys Davids	1.00
Buddhist Catechism (H. S. Olcott)	.40
Blossom and the Fruit, M. C. Cloth, $1.00; paper,	.40
Buddhist Diet Book	.50
Christos, J. D. Buck	.75
Divine Pymander, Hermes Trismegistus	3.00
Discourses on the Bhagavad Gita, Subba Row	.75

Yoga Aphorisms of Patanjali, American edition. Flexible.............. .80

Any of the above books, as well as the periodicals below, may be obtained by remitting the price to Secretary Pacific Coast Theosophic Corporation, Mercantile Library Building, San Francisco.

. Periodicals.

Subscriptions will be received for the following Magazines:

Price per annum.

"The Path,"..	$2.00
"Lucifer,"..	4.40
"The Theosophist,"..	5.00
"Theosophical Siftings,"..	1.25
"Pacific Theosophist, '..	1.00

THE
OCEAN ⚛ OF ⚛ THEOSOPHY
—BY—
WM. Q. JUDGE, F. T. S.

This work is designed to give the general reader some knowlege of the most important Theosophical Doctrines, and at the same time it will be of great value to students in the Theosophical Society. It contains seventeen chapters and gives a clear idea of the fundamental principles of the Wisdom Religion. The following is a brief synopsis of the book:

Chapter I deals with the general aspects of Theosophy, and that ever-interesting subject, the MASTERS....Chap. II—Is a concise presentation of Evolution and its records in ancient chronologies....Chap. III—Deals with our Earth more particularly—shows its septenary nature, and its relation to other planets of our plane....Chap. IV—Applies this septenary division to man, and deals with his "Principles" in a general way....Chap V—Takes up the Body and Astral Body....Chap. VI—Examines the nature of Kama....Chap. VII— Of Manas, or the Thinking Principle; all together, forming, perhaps, the clearest explanation yet written of the nature and functions of these Principles.... Chaps. VIII, IX and X deal with Reincarnation and its evidences....Chap. XI— With Karma....Chaps. XII and XIII—With Post-Mortem Existence.... Chap. XIV—With Cycles....Chap. XV—With the Derivation of Man, the Apes, etc....Chaps. XVI and XVII—With Psychic Force, "Spiritualism," and allied topics.

Cloth, $1.00; paper, 50c.

Mailed, post-paid, on receipt of price..

THE PATH,

144 Madison Avenue, New York.

Or, THE P. C. COMMITTEE, Mercantile Library Building, San Francisco.